ROCK OF FREEDOM

THE STORY OF
THE PLYMOUTH COLONY

Noel B. Gerson

SAPERE
BOOKS

ROCK OF FREEDOM

Published by Sapere Books.

20 Windermere Drive, Leeds, England, LS17 7UZ,
United Kingdom

saperebooks.com

ISBN: 978-1-80055-093-3

For
Peggy and Susan Russell

TABLE OF CONTENTS

1

There was no sound in the vast, black expanse of wilderness but the faint, steady drip of raindrops falling from pines and birches, cedars and poplars and firs. Gradually the dark clouds hovering over the crescent of land on which Plymouth Colony was built began to roll away. A few stars appeared, and it was probable that the last Friday in August, 1623, would be fair.

The young sentry stationed at the gate of the stockade that marked the limits of the town yawned and absently rubbed his left hand on his threadbare woolen breeches. He rested his heavy musket on the ground, leaning the barrel against the wooden palisade. Stretching and yawning again, he wished daylight would come, for the night seemed endless. He would have to go to work as soon as he ate breakfast, of course; there were too few men in Plymouth to allow a sentinel the luxury of sleep after ten hours on guard duty. But it would be a relief to be active after wasting the night.

Suddenly there was a distinct, crackling sound in the underbrush beyond the fields of growing corn. The sentry froze, then reached hastily for his musket.

The noise became clearer, and a cold, tingling fear crept up the sentry's spine. All of the Indian nations of Cape Cod were supposedly at peace with Plymouth, but the leaders of the colony had been saying for weeks that the quiet was deceptive. Perhaps the savages were intending to launch their long-threatened assault on the little colony here and now.

The sentry cocked his musket, and the loud, metallic click of the hammer reassured him.

The other young guard who was standing night duty came up beside him. They had been trained not to speak in an emergency such as this, so both remained silent as they stared off at the tangled mass of tree branches, bushes and weeds. Someone — or something — was lurking in the forest, but they could see nothing. Inside the town a dog barked, then howled.

The sentries caught a glimpse of a small animal that appeared in the open for an instant but vanished when it caught the scent of men. The taller of the guards relaxed and wiped a film of perspiration from his forehead. "If I'd known there was a porcupine or a raccoon out yonder, wanting to nibble our corn, I could have shot it," he said. "We'd have had a meat stew for breakfast."

His companion was unconcerned. "Porcupines and raccoons are too small."

"Some meat is better than none," the taller of the pair replied bleakly.

Both glanced involuntarily in the direction of the sheds where bags of grain, smoked venison and pickled cod were stored. There was no need for further comment. Both knew that, although there was a supply of food in the sheds, it wasn't enough for the winter months. And the sentries, like everyone else in Plymouth, couldn't remember when they had last eaten a truly filling meal.

Gaunt and hungry, they returned to their posts, still vigilant, waiting for the slightest sound that would indicate an impending Indian attack.

Dawn came, and the two-and-one-half-year-old colony on the edge of the untamed wilderness began to stir. Children raced down the hill and across the rocks to the beach for a quick swim, but did not return empty-handed. They brought mussels and clams to their parents, who needed every scrap of food to help swell meager larders. Housewives carefully measured small quantities of cornmeal into bowls, then added water to make a batter. Husbands built up fires that had been banked during the night, and heated large, flat stones in the flames. Pancakes would be made by dropping batter onto the stones, for there was no butter or other shortening in Plymouth. Frying pans were virtually useless.

Governor William Bradford, a lean, suntanned man of thirty-four, sat before the fire in his own hearth, grilling a small trout. He ate the fish quickly, concentrating on other matters, for the trout, which was all he would eat for breakfast, merely whetted his appetite.

Bradford posted the day's work schedule outside his small house. Then he slung his musket over his shoulder and, picking up a rake and shovel, started off down the Street toward the palisade and the fields beyond it. Even the Governor was forced to engage in hard physical labor, for starvation was a constant threat.

"William!" Someone hailed Bradford from the entrance of a larger house, located at the corner of the Street and the Road, the village's two thoroughfares.

The Governor stopped, then smiled when he saw gray haired Elder Brewster, the community's religious leader, who was acting as a minister until Pastor John Robinson came from Holland to join his flock.

Brewster did not return the smile. "You're too thin," he said severely. "Mary and I are worried about you."

Bradford shrugged. "It's my duty to set an example. We've got to fill the storage sheds so that there will be enough to eat this winter."

Elder Brewster raised an eyebrow. "Are you so afraid that no ships will come from England?"

The Governor's hazel eyes became hard. "How often have we been promised supplies from England, only to be disappointed?" he demanded. "If we hope to survive, we can rely only on ourselves!"

"We must rely on the Lord, too," Brewster reminded him.

Bradford accepted the reprimand with good grace, but was still worried. "If our financial supporters in London don't help us soon, we'll have to work even harder. I'm thinking of making out schedules for the Sabbath."

The Elder was shocked. "But the Sabbath is sacred!"

Bradford's expression did not change. "We wanted our freedom," he said flatly, "and we've won it. But the price of liberty is high." Not waiting for a reply, he walked past the palisade into the fields. The future of Plymouth depended on the harvest that the crops of corn and beans would yield. Keeping his musket close beside him in case of an Indian attack, he started to pull weeds.

The two men who were doing guard duty during daylight hours watched him for a few moments from the Fort. The largest and strongest building in the village, it stood at the crest of Town Hill, and was used as a meeting place, church and dining hall when not being utilized for military purposes. One of the sentries grinned and shook his head. Luckily for Plymouth, William Bradford's energy was inexhaustible.

Then the young man transferred his attention to the sea and silently nudged his companion. Far out in the Atlantic they saw a tiny speck, almost invisible on the horizon. They stared at it uneasily, and eventually were able to make out the shape of a large, rectangular sail.

The sentry in charge ran down into the town to the widower's hut occupied by Captain Miles Standish, the colony's hired military leader. A short, stocky man with a face burned a reddish color by the sun and wind, Standish listened intently to the report. Losing no time, he donned his breastplate, pulled his heavy steel helmet onto his head and, grasping his sword, hurried up to the Fort.

Two ships were plainly visible on the horizon now. One appeared to be a large vessel of approximately one hundred and fifty tons, and the other was about one-third her size. They were sailing together, and there was no doubt that they were headed in the direction of Plymouth.

Standish studied them through an enlarging glass, and grasped his sword more tightly with his free hand when he saw cannon on the decks of both vessels.

"Sound the alarm!" he directed.

The early morning quiet was shattered by a volley of musket fire.

All ordinary activity stopped at once.

The alert aroused the whole community. Men snatched the firearms they kept beside them day and night, and ran to the posts they had been assigned when danger threatened. Some went to the palisade, others raced to the Fort. Those who were working in the fields beyond the high, wooden wall dashed back into the town, and Bradford closed the gate, then slid a solid bolt of heavy oak into place.

In the first minutes, no one quite knew the source of potential danger, but every woman, every child, was ready to join the men in the Fort if it proved necessary. The people of Plymouth were prepared to resist their enemies to the last breath. After living so near to death for so long, after surviving famine and disease, fierce storms and the hot hatred of savage barbarians, the colonists were not afraid.

Bradford was one of the first to reach the Fort, and immediately joined Standish.

The Captain, tense in times of danger but always reliable, pointed toward the sails, which were growing larger with each passing moment.

Bradford was simultaneously worried and relieved. "There won't be an Indian attack," he said, but knew that an even worse danger threatened.

Standish nodded soberly. "Those ships might be manned by pirates." Unscrupulous rogues from the West Indian Islands, renegade Englishmen who sank other ships on the high seas, were the scourge of the New World. A flotilla of these scoundrels had attacked a colony to the south, in Virginia, several years earlier, and had killed many of the settlers, looted storehouses and burned homes before being forced to withdraw.

Bradford drew a deep breath. "They may be Frenchmen," he said, his eyes narrowing. There was a strong possibility that the government of France had sent an official expedition of soldiers and sailors to capture and occupy a colony established by the English, France's ancient foe. Plymouth was a particularly tempting target, for most of her inhabitants were outcasts, people whose religious beliefs had caused them to be banished from their native land by King James I. If they were attacked by a foreign power, they could not appeal to London for help. They stood alone.

Still vigilant, Bradford relaxed slightly. "There's a chance, a slim chance, that the ships are friendly," he declared.

The men clustered behind him listened eagerly. They all remembered that in the spring a trading ship from England

14

had put into Plymouth with word that a new expedition would set out for Plymouth soon. According to that report, scores of new settlers were coming, among them relatives who had remained behind when the original pioneers had crossed the Atlantic on the *Mayflower* in 1620.

Bradford refrained from saying that a large company of new colonists would make the plight of the settlement even more hazardous. The food shortage was so severe that he had no idea how dozens more men, women and children would be fed. No matter whether there were friends or enemies on board the ships, the future was bleak.

But he could not wait idly. Standish was watching him, waiting for an order.

They exchanged a quick glance, and understood each other so well that words were unnecessary. Men who had lived at death's door for nearly three years knew instinctively that every risk had to be reduced to a minimum.

"Man that cannon!" Standish directed.

Eight colonists hauled, shoved and pulled the ancient saker, Plymouth's only cannon, toward one of the open gunports that faced the harbor. A mammoth, clumsy weapon, the saker was a muzzle-loader, difficult to aim and dangerous to use. On the few occasions when it had been fired, chiefly to impress Cape Cod Indians, everyone had been in mortal fear it would burst at the seams and explode.

Such a danger existed now, but there was no choice. Precious gunpowder was poured down the cannon's throat, then a heavy iron ball was rammed home. Standish aimed the saker himself, changing the elevation of the barrel until he felt reasonably sure that a shot would land at the entrance to the harbor. If the strangers proved to be enemies, even one shot could severely damage the larger of the ships.

The Governor peered down the barrel, and was satisfied.

Men quietly loaded and checked their muskets, buckled on swords and slid bone-handled knives into their boot tops. Everyone was prepared to die, if need be, to preserve a way of life that was dear.

Bradford beckoned to two boys who were too young to join the fighting force. "Run down into the town," he ordered, "and bring all of the women and children here! Hurry!"

Soon the wives and mothers of Plymouth were toiling up the slopes of Town Hill, shepherding their young. The self-discipline was remarkable. Not one child cried, and all remained silent. They filed into the Fort and took their places on the crude benches of unpainted wood that were ordinarily used by worshippers on the Sabbath. There was no panic.

The larger of the ships tacked and headed toward the harbor. Those who were staring out of the glassless windows saw that she carried five sails. The smaller vessel, laboring in her wake, had two sails, and was having difficulty keeping up the same, swift pace. Bradford was able to make out several figures on the main deck of the lead ship, but could not tell whether they were soldiers in uniform.

The tension continued to mount, and soon became almost unbearable. Bradford broke the silence. "Captain Standish," he said crisply, "run up our flag."

The colony's pennant, a hand-sewn English ensign, was taken from a cupboard, unfolded and tied to a length of braided vine that served as a rope. It was hoisted to the top of a pole, the trunk of a large poplar, that had been erected on the roof of the Fort.

Now, if the strangers were friendly, they would identify themselves.

There was a stir on the quarterdeck of the larger ship, then a banner was hauled to the topgallants, where it unfurled and snapped in the breeze. The flag was that of England!

The men in the Fort cheered, and the younger children began to shout. A few of the women wept, and others offered quiet prayers of thanks. The danger, it appeared, had passed.

The colonists hurried down to the beach, with Governor Bradford in the lead. He studied the ships intently, and when he caught sight of women on the decks of both, he knew that the vessels truly were carrying new colonists. Neither French naval vessels nor buccaneers from the West Indian Islands traveled with women on board. The ships undoubtedly were bringing recruits from the Separatist exile community in Holland and, perhaps, kindred souls from England.

The one-hundred-and-fifty-ton brig sailed into Plymouth harbor, and the fifty or sixty men and women crowding close to the rail on her main deck waved energetically. Those on shore cheered, and the sound rolled across the harbor.

Making a supreme effort not to think about the now-critical problem of obtaining enough food for everyone, Bradford dared to hope that the woman he had loved since he had been a boy in Yorkshire was a passenger on one of the ships. She was a widow, he was a widower, and after years of heartache they were free to marry at last.

Several boats were lowered from the brig into the water; people climbed down swaying rope ladders into them, and they started toward the shore. The crew of the captain's gig pulled hard at the oars, and when it drew close to the beach, several young men sprinted into the shallow water to haul it up onto the rocks.

Gentle Sam Fuller, whose knowledge of drugs and native herbs had caused him to be pressed into service as Plymouth's physician, cried out in startled ecstasy. Then he ran toward the boat, laughing and crying at the same time. His friends smiled delightedly when they saw that the lone woman seated in the stern was his wife. She was weeping, too, and was so overcome that she could not speak when her husband took her in his arms.

Governor Bradford concentrated his attention on the tall, uniformed officer who approached him.

"Governor Bradford? Captain William Peirce, master of the *Anne*, out of London. I bring you sixty-one passengers from Holland and England, and there are thirty-two more on the *Little James*, which crossed the Atlantic with us."

Bradford shook hands cordially, but there was a note of uncertainty in his voice. "I'm delighted to see you, Captain. I can only hope we'll be able to absorb so many newcomers."

Peirce laughed and handed him a folded sheet of paper. "You'll be happier to see my manifest than to chat with me."

Bradford became slightly giddy as he scanned a long list. The merchant adventurers in London, who supported the colony financially, had opened their purses freely and had sent him even more than he asked. He could scarcely believe what he read:

100 Barrels of Beef
100 Barrels of White Flour
50 Bags of Gunpowder
100 Barrels of Salt Pork
1 Saker Cannon
2 Small Cannon
3 Bags of Seed: Peas, Beans
1 Bag of Onions, suitable for planting
1 Bag of Carrots, suitable for planting
300 Bolts of Wool (Gray)

20 Bolts of Wool (White)
50 Bolts of Corduroy (Gray)
30 Bolts of Corduroy (Black)
100 Bolts of Sheer Lawn Linen (White)
40 Bolts of Heavy Linen (White)
70½ Bales of Shoe Leather

In all, Peirce added, the *Anne* was carrying more than sixty tons of merchandise. Plymouth would have more than enough food and clothing, more than enough ammunition to protect her. Another ten tons, including tools, muskets — and several packets of badly needed sewing needles for the women — were in the hold of the *Little James*. Of even greater importance was the fact that that ship would be left at Plymouth for the colonists' permanent use.

Bradford was stunned. Possession of the sleek vessel, strong enough to have crossed the Atlantic and more than sturdy enough for use in New World waters, instantly solved all of Plymouth's fishing problems. It would be possible to make long voyages of exploration up and down the coast, too. And, in time, as other permanent settlements came into being, the colonists could visit them in the ship. The merchant adventurers had displayed remarkable forethought. Never again would Plymouth tremble on the brink of starvation. Never again would the colony be cut off from the rest of the civilized world for long, lonely months.

"The Lord has provided for us," Bradford murmured. "All glory to God."

Peirce moved off discreetly, and as the boats landed passengers, the Governor recovered his poise in time to greet the new arrivals.

At last, after shaking hands with scores of old friends and new acquaintances, he found the woman he was seeking, Alice

Carpenter Southworth. Fatigue showed in her face after the long voyage, but she was still lovely. Her strength and serenity, he thought, were becoming more pronounced as she grew older, and maturity gave her great dignity. She was dressed in a pale gray gown of wool. Significantly, her head was bare. She wore neither the starched white muslin cap of a married woman nor the black one of a widow. Spots of color appeared in her cheeks, and she started to curtsy, but Bradford hastily lifted her to her feet, and they embraced. The long, cruel years of separation were ended.

Reluctantly he left her, for the Governor's duties required his attention. The immigrants were given temporary quarters. Farm sites were to be allotted to every man, and each given land for a house. Before homes were constructed it would be necessary to build new, huge storage sheds for the cargo that was being carried ashore.

The dazed settlers stared in wonder at the bountiful provisions, the many items that meant the difference between comfort and hardship on the edge of a vast, barbaric wilderness. There were, the women saw, three spinning wheels in the cargo. Their construction was so simple that soon every home in Plymouth would have its own loom.

Several large bags, each wrapped in layers of protective cloth, were the most precious of the supplies. These were wheat seeds and oats, rye and barley. There were enough peas and other vegetables to insure that a large, diversified crop could be planted the following spring.

The next day each of the newly arrived men listened to Bradford read the document known as the Mayflower Compact. This simple declaration, which had been drawn up by the original settlers on board the *Mayflower*, guaranteed a separation of church and state, and promised freedom of worship to all, regardless of their beliefs.

Each newcomer swore he would uphold its principles. He was also asked to swear he would obey the laws the colonists had made to govern themselves and to join the militia. As soon as he agreed, he was granted the full privileges of citizenship.

When the ceremonies were completed, cooking fires were lighted on the beach for a great feast. But before anyone ate, the entire community — established settlers and newcomers alike — walked up to the Fort. Reunited families sat together, wives clung to their husbands' arms, and the excited children, seeing the solemn faces of the adults, became quiet.

Elder Brewster offered a prayer of deep gratitude to the Almighty for the blessings showered on Plymouth. The entire congregation fervently joined in.

Then Governor Bradford stood. He walked slowly to the open windows that looked out at the vast expanse of forest, a solid green mass that stretched out to meet the horizon. "When we who came here on the *Mayflower* first saw the wilderness," he said, "we were uneasy. But the challenge was so great that we soon forgot our fears. And those who wanted to conquer the wilderness quickly learned their error.

"The New World is so enormous that the combined armies of England and the nations of continental Europe could not subdue it.

"We have learned to think in terms of a different sort of challenge, one that will not change for hundreds of years." He paused and looked intently at his audience. "Men must learn to live in harmony with this land, to utilize her resources for their benefit. Those who abuse or resist her will be crushed, but those who make a genuine effort to understand her discover that she yields her fruits to them with a generous hand."

The veteran settlers, suntanned and hard-muscled, nodded in agreement. Nowhere on earth was the soil richer, nowhere was the water clearer or the air more bracing. Only vaguely aware that they were pioneers who were shaping the destiny of the mightiest nation on earth, they nevertheless sensed that they were the founders of a new breed.

"People who think the wilderness is hostile are mistaken," Bradford said. "There is great tranquility here, as you who are new will find as soon as you adjust to our ways. The spirit of America insists that everyone must rely on himself.

"America demands strength, and now that our immediate needs have been filled, we shall give her what she wants and needs. Our first battles have been fought and won by men and women of courage. That courage will be inherited and accepted as a tradition by future generations. We cannot fail now, because we have refused to accept failure.

"This land will become truly great, for her foundation rests upon a rock of freedom. Neither time, nor the elements, nor enemies of liberty, will destroy that freedom.

"This day, this month, this year, will in the centuries ahead be remembered as a turning point, for a new era has dawned."

2

What caused a little band of stubborn, idealistic Englishmen to venture thousands of miles from home in order to set up their own community in the wilds of an unknown continent?

What forces impelled these quiet farmers and merchants, most of them natives of rural Yorkshire, Lincolnshire and Nottinghamshire, to take part in one of mankind's greatest epic adventures?

Were they, as they have been judged by history, almost larger-than-life heroes and heroines? Or were they, as their own generation believed, stiff-necked fools and madmen?

Who were these Separatists, or Pilgrims as they have since been called?

Their story really began one hundred years before their voyage to the shores of Cape Cod. It started during the reign of England's most popular monarch, Henry VIII, who founded the Church of England. His break with the Roman Catholic faith marked the inauguration of the Reformation in England.

Henry's successors, his son and two daughters, continued the struggle. Edward VI was a Protestant, Queen Mary was a Catholic, Queen Elizabeth I was a Protestant. In the years they ruled, innocent people were made to suffer because of their religious beliefs.

When James I, who was already king of Scotland, ascended to the throne of England in 1603, it appeared as though the troubled land would enjoy an era of peace for the first time in almost seventy-five years. James was a devout Protestant, much interested in religion. It was he who appointed a commission of the greatest scholars in the British Isles, linguists and historians and churchmen, to make a new translation of the Holy Bible from Hebrew and Greek into English. That work, known as the King James Bible, is still used today.

But James was a moody, suspicious man, sometimes wise, more often foolish. Elizabeth had taken care to leave religious matters in the hands of her bishops and had not made an issue of her father's claim that he must be recognized as the active head of the Church of England. It was enough, she thought, that she should hold the title, and she had no desire to wield real authority in religious affairs.

James felt otherwise. Soon after he became king of England, he demanded that all citizens admit he was their supreme religious leader. Most obeyed, for people were weary of religious strife. And the vast majority felt they were merely making a gesture toward the Crown. They were certain that, in practice, James would follow Elizabeth's custom and let the bishops decide matters of ecclesiastical concern.

But a tiny minority in the Midlands disagreed. These prosperous farmers and merchants, residents of Yorkshire, Lincolnshire and Nottinghamshire, had been buffeted for many years by opposing religious winds. They were honest and sober, God-fearing men and women who worshipped the Almighty piously, humbly. It was their deepest conviction that, although man should swear loyalty to the king in temporal matters, he owed allegiance only to God in his religious beliefs.

The group was so small that, at first, King James paid little attention to its opposition. His bailiffs and other officials in the Midland counties explained to the rebels that James was a kindly man, but a firm master, and that he meant what he said. The dissenters refused to budge.

Gradually they banded together, and called themselves Separatists. They were, quite literally, Protestants who had deliberately separated themselves from the Church of England.

John Robinson was their pastor, and nowhere in the British Isles was there a more devoted congregation. Sabbath services lasted for many hours, and no work was done on the Sabbath. Men constantly searched their own hearts and minds for flaws, for errors, and made conscientious attempts to improve themselves. They helped each other in a spirit of fellowship, and a closely knit group developed. They studied the Bible, pondered its meaning and, making a sincere effort to live their faith, believed they walked close to God.

Had the King ignored their activities, few Englishmen would have known of the Separatists' existence. But James was outraged, for he believed that kings ruled by Divine right. In other words, he was convinced that whatever ruling he might make, on any matter, was automatically sanctioned by the Almighty. A monarch holding these views could not tolerate the rebellion of any group, even one as small as the band of Separatists.

It was James' personal inclination to throw the Separatists into prison, perhaps behead them. But his advisers were more cautious. They knew, from England's previous history, that when one man was executed for his religious beliefs, he immediately became a martyr in the eyes of others, and soon a dozen new converts appeared in his place. So it was better, the Crown's ministers thought, to move slowly against the Separatists, to apply stronger and stronger pressure against them. Eventually they would give in.

William Brewster of Yorkshire, a lay leader of the Separatist church, was employed by the government as the postmaster of the Austerfield-Scrooby district, a position of considerable importance. He was the first to feel the King's wrath.

One day early in the year 1607, when the snow was piled high on the streets of Austerfield, Brewster sat in his office, working quietly. A clerk informed him that a visitor of importance had come to see him, so he stood, smoothing his official coat of dark red, resplendent with silver buttons.

A man with a small, pointed beard, who was dressed in a suit of black velvet, came into the room. Scarcely bothering to glance at his host, he stamped snow from his boots, threw back his long cloak and stood before the fire in the hearth, warming himself.

"How may I serve you, sir?" Brewster asked courteously.

The visitor drew a parchment scroll from his belt and handed it to the postmaster.

Brewster unrolled the document and immediately recognized the royal seal. Master Guy Henry, he read, held a position as confidential agent for the Crown and enjoyed the personal trust of King James. Impressed but not awed, Brewster waited for the rude stranger to speak.

"You're a troublemaker." Henry rubbed his hands together, then tugged at his beard.

"My books are in order," Brewster replied calmly. "We sort and deliver the mail as rapidly as we receive it, and we've had no complaints."

The confidential agent laughed harshly. "Half the citizens of Yorkshire have complained about you," he declared vigorously. "Your religious views offend them."

Brewster refused to be bullied. "My faith is my own," he said. "I've never forced my convictions on anyone else, and they don't interfere with my work."

"They offend King James!"

26

"I'm flattered that the King has heard of me." Brewster continued to hold his ground.

Henry looked him up and down, slowly, insolently. "Does life mean so little to you that you want to be hanged?"

"What crime have I committed?"

"You refused to acknowledge King James as your master in all things."

"I serve him to the best of my ability, and I obey his civil laws."

"You take his silver, which supports you and your family. But you refuse to serve him." The confidential agent drew a glittering poniard from his belt.

Brewster wondered whether he would have to defend himself physically. He moved a casual step or two closer to the side of the hearth, where an iron poker stood within reach.

"I'm here to give you your last chance," Henry told him, gesturing menacingly with the double-edged knife. "If you'll abandon your foolish, rebellious ways, no harm will come to you. But if you insist on remaining a member of a traitorous church, I've been authorized to dismiss you from your post at once."

"Nothing can force me to give up my membership in the Separatist church!" Brewster raised his voice for the first time.

"Then get out!" Henry took a step toward him.

Brewster reached for the iron poker.

The confidential agent laughed. "I wouldn't dirty my hands with your sort. There are others who will beat you until you fall to your knees and beg the King's forgiveness."

"I kneel only before the altar of the Lord."

Henry was exasperated. "I haven't come all the way from London to listen to your mealy-mouthed drivel. You've been employed by the Crown, but you refuse to acknowledge King

James as the head of your church. You're dismissed from your office. Take your personal belongings and go."

Brewster moved to a small cabinet and began to throw quill pens and seals, his Bible and a variety of odds and ends into a box. "I intend to lodge an official protest," he declared, not losing his dignity.

"You're denied the privilege!"

"Privilege, Master Henry? It's my right."

"Traitors have no rights."

Brewster put on his hat and adjusted his cloak over his shoulders. "Neither you nor any other man — including King James himself — can frighten me," he said as he started toward the door.

Henry's harsh voice echoed in the corridor. "It's treason to preach the separation of church and state. And unless you change your ways, Brewster, you'll end your life swinging from a gibbet!"

William Brewster squared his shoulders as the cold air stung his face. He inhaled deeply, then started off through the snow toward his house. He had a wife and children to feed, and his future suddenly was bleak. But he had acted according to the dictates of his conscience, and held his head high.

Other Separatists soon felt the strong royal pressure, too.

George and Thomas Morton were members of a wealthy Roman Catholic family from Yorkshire who became attracted to the Separatist cause and joined the church. George was a merchant, Thomas a farmer, and both owned considerable property. A Crown tax assessor called on them, and their annual taxes were tripled. They filed complaints through the courts, but their cases were postponed so many times that they knew they would never obtain justice. Their neighbors, who owned almost identical property, continued to pay taxes at the old rate.

John Carver, of Doncaster, Yorkshire, was one of the few members of the patrician class who found Separatism attractive. He lived off his large income, part of which came from several small manufacturing plants. There was a stir in the area when he formally joined the Separatist church, and a few days later he was summoned to York by Crown attorneys, who demanded to see his titles to various of his properties. The lawyers sadly shook their heads, told him that his papers were not in order and that, in reality, he probably did not own the various business enterprises, after all.

Francis Cooke, a young farm owner, had inherited his land from his father in a direct line of descent. But the Crown bailiffs claimed that Cooke, Senior, had never lived up to the financial obligations he had owed to Queen Elizabeth, and fined the son such a huge sum that he was unable to pay even a portion of it. So they threatened to confiscate the entire property.

Not all of the Separatists were men of substance, however. Alexander Carpenter was a poor tenant farmer in Yorkshire. He had a wife and three daughters, and although he was a devout member of the church, he tried to live cautiously so he would not bring the royal wrath down on his head. But his daughters made no secret of their faith, and all were courted by bachelors in the group. The nobleman from whom Carpenter rented his farm warned him that he and his family would have to worship more discreetly or be forced to move elsewhere.

Roger White, Pastor Robinson's brother-in-law, was apprenticed to a weaver. William Buckrum was a carpenter, and young Ralph Tickens, a native of London, was apprenticed to a maker of looking glasses. They, together with Edward

Southworth, a silk maker, and other younger members of the group, were considered too unimportant to merit the attention of the Crown authorities.

But the case of seventeen-year-old William Bradford of Austerfield was somewhat different. He was an orphan who owned a large farm left to him by his father. It was being held for him by his uncles, with whom he lived. As he was someone who would come into property, the bailiffs were interested in him.

He found it difficult to make up his own mind. Pastor Robinson warned the Separatists they would be forced to decide, in the immediate future, whether their religion meant more to them than their future in England. Brewster, whom Bradford regarded as a foster father, urged the boy to remain firm in his convictions and not waver.

Bradford watched the coming storm gather force. Separatists were forbidden to hold worship services in churches, and had to meet in barns, as private homes were too small and cramped. Only one final move remained in the sly game King James was playing. As all England knew, soon he would sign an official decree commanding the religious rebels to return to the fold of the Church of England.

If they refused, they would become traitors and outlaws. Members of the band would be sent to prison, and the leaders would surely hang.

Robinson wanted to avoid that terrible dilemma. He proposed that his parishioners leave England and take up residence in Holland, where sanctuary was granted to the persecuted of any faith. The Dutch Reformed Church, a semi-official organization, was one of the most liberal in Europe, and the whole country was known to be tolerant. Dutch Reformed clergymen with whom Robinson corresponded

accept him as my temporal superior. I'll obey his civil laws. I'll serve in his army. And I'll pay my taxes to the collectors who wear his uniform. But I'll kneel before no man, regardless of whether he calls himself king or bishop."

Robert's high-pitched laugh sounded blasphemous. "When Elizabeth was on the throne, papists were sent to prison and died by the hundreds. There may be a few in the country who still would prostrate themselves before the altars of Rome, but they've learned to keep their ideas to themselves. It's the Separatists who are troubling the waters now, and King James won't tolerate their defiance. So don't prattle about freedom to worship as you please, lad. Not in England."

"Members of the Separatist church hold the view," William replied doggedly, "that we'll obey the King in secular matters. But the only spiritual authority we recognize is that of God Himself. We hold that church and state are separate, not united."

"Do your philosophers and learned men of Scrooby," Robert asked sarcastically, "think themselves so wise, so powerful that they dare oppose decrees approved by the Privy Council and signed by the King? Are they so short-sighted they think they can break the royal seal and escape punishment?"

"Laws are made by men, Uncle Robert, and the leaders of our congregation will obey the law in all matters that pertain to men. But no earthly potentate, no bishop of a state church and no government minister can tell them how to worship. They walk with God, and so do I."

The men glanced at each other briefly, and Robert's helpless shrug indicated that nothing more could be said or done. He stamped out of the kitchen without speaking again, and his brother followed him.

William Bradford was startled when he suddenly realized he had made his decision without consciously knowing it.

The opposition of his uncles had solidified his own thinking, and his future was settled. He would go with the Separatists to Holland.

He realized he would be leaving England without a penny to his name. The rich land his father had left him would be seized by the Crown and, in all probability, sold to his uncles for a token sum. And it was quite possible he would never see Alice Carpenter again.

Come what may, the die was cast.

One morning in mid-November, 1607, a small crowd of curious citizens gathered on the banks of the Witham River and watched cargo being loaded onto the Dutch schooner *Katje*. The passengers, awaiting their turn to go aboard the ship, stood a short distance away and self-protectively pretended to be unaware of the throng. But they apparently had nothing to fear, for the citizens of the Lincolnshire town of Boston were accustomed to the sight of departing Separatists. Four loads had put out through the Wash into the North Sea in recent weeks, and the men and women who preferred to give up their native land for the sake of what they considered religious freedom were no longer a novelty.

This group was somewhat different, in part because it was the last scheduled to depart. Even more important, the most prominent of the Separatist leaders were members of the party. The principal bailiff of Lincolnshire, accompanied by more than a score of his deputies, was on hand to see them off. No attempt was made to hinder those who were leaving. On the contrary, the authorities were pleased to see the troublemakers go.

Each was asked the same questions by a deputy bailiff:

"Are you leaving England of your own free will?"

"Do you know that you are giving up English citizenship, which you cannot regain until such time as you are willing to acknowledge the spiritual supremacy of His Majesty?"

"Do you understand that you may not set foot again on the soil of England, Scotland and Wales until such time as you freely acknowledge the spiritual supremacy of His Majesty?"

The break with the familiar world the Separatists had always known seemed suddenly violent, irrevocable, but not one member of the congregation faltered. All, men and women alike, gave their replies in clear, firm voices. Pastor Robinson was the first, then William Brewster; then each of the others stepped forward. The bailiffs addressed them in mocking tones, and it was obvious that the Crown officials thought that people were mad who willingly abandoned homes and property for the sake of what seemed like a vague principle.

But not one of the Separatists hesitated. And if the spectators expected to see a man suddenly recoil or a woman burst into tears, they were disappointed. The last of the cargo had been stored in the hold of the *Katje*, and when the legal formalities were completed, Pastor Robinson led his flock across a narrow plank of wood onto the deck of the schooner. Barring the totally unexpected, most of the Separatists had stood for the last time on the soil of their native England.

The crowd was no longer able to restrain itself. Several men began to boo, and catcalls added to the din. A burly hostler shook his fist at the quiet, soberly dressed men and women who stood now on the main deck of the *Katje*. A longshoreman cursed.

"Traitors!" A harsh voice rose above the hubbub.

Others picked up the cry.

Young William Bradford stood on the deck, his fists clenched, and looked as though he would climb onto the rail, then leap ashore.

Brewster placed a restraining hand on his shoulder. "Don't," he said. "There are times when a man must fight, and there are times when common sense and dignity require him to tolerate abuse."

Slowly, reluctantly, Bradford relaxed.

The captain of the schooner shouted an order, and the *Katje* weighed anchor. Her sails filling, she gathered speed as she sailed down the Witham toward the Wash, the open sea and Holland.

"We are Pilgrims," Pastor Robinson declared. "Many of us are destitute, and we have no friends in Leyden and Amsterdam who will give us work. But we are not afraid of an alien land. Our consciences have told us what to do. Our beliefs mean more to us than gold or silver. My friends, we will live to see a brighter day."

3

By 1617, ten years after the first Separatist refugees had left England, two colonies were solidly established in Holland. There were about three hundred Separatists living in Leyden; the group in Amsterdam was somewhat smaller. Newcomers arrived occasionally, with chilling stories of the persecution that the faithful were suffering at home. Men suspected of Separatist sympathies were arrested, thrown into dungeons and held for long months without trial. Crown bailiffs urged townspeople to stone and mock the women. A royal decree stated that the children of Separatists could not attend schools, and they had to be taught at home.

Everyone was grateful for the sanctuary offered by the Dutch, but life was not easy. It was difficult to find work, and most of the men considered themselves fortunate if they obtained employment as common laborers. But no one complained, and few envied the handful who had become successful. One of this small group was William Bradford, who was the prosperous owner of a clothmaking plant.

Twenty-eight years old now, he had become one of the leaders of the Pilgrim community, and was a full-fledged citizen of Leyden. He had recovered, at least outwardly, from the shock he had sustained when Alice Carpenter's father had married her, against her will, to Edward Southworth of London, who worshipped as a Separatist in the privacy of his own humble home.

Refusing to give in to despair, Bradford had married, too. His wife, Dorothy May, the daughter of a Separatist couple living in Amsterdam, had become his bride at the age of sixteen. Still a child in many ways, she was a strange, moody girl, and too late Bradford discovered that she cared neither for him nor for the Separatist cause that meant so much to him. Even their baby, John, had failed to arouse her from the depths of ever-present gloom. Bradford tried to make the best of the situation.

One cold December night in 1617, the men were called to an unexpected, emergency meeting at the house of William Brewster. None of them knew why they had been summoned. Bradford, walking to his old friend's house through the snow-laden streets with Edward Winslow, an energetic young man in his early twenties, refused to speculate.

"Pastor Robinson will tell us all we need to know," he said. "If he asks for another contribution for those who are in want, I'll gladly pay my share."

The two men walked past the huge, medieval buildings of the city's great university, then turned onto a twisting lane so narrow that Winslow had to fall behind his companion. Suddenly they found their path blocked by three men carrying heavy staffs, and they stopped abruptly. Bradford owned a sword and pistol, but was carrying neither, for Leyden was a quiet place, and violence there was rare.

"Robbers!" Winslow exclaimed.

The leader of the trio pointed his thick staff at Bradford. "You're the robber," he said in heavily accented English. "You deprive honest Hollanders of work."

Bradford peered at him in the dark and recognized a journeyman weaver who had applied for a position at his plant a few days earlier. "I'm a citizen here, as you are," he replied calmly. "I pay my taxes and carry my full share of the burden in every way."

The weaver stubbornly shook his head. "You pay wages to five clothmakers. All of them are English. Why do you refuse to give work to honest Dutchmen?"

Bradford braced himself for trouble, but muttered under his breath as Winslow stepped forward, "Don't crowd me, Edward. I can handle this."

The weaver raised his staff high, then brought it down swiftly, aiming at the Englishman's head.

Bradford side-stepped and, at the same moment, caught the end of the staff. Giving his opponent no time to recover from his surprise, he twisted and pulled the stick in the same motion, and the weaver lost his grip.

Armed now, Bradford struck hard. He jabbed the pole at the weaver, who took the blow in the pit of his stomach and staggered back against his companions, gasping. There was virtually no room to maneuver in the alley, and Bradford shrewdly used the lack of space to his advantage. Neither of the other Hollanders could reach past the weaver to hit him with their staffs, but he had complete freedom of movement.

He forced the men to drop their weapons, and when they realized their position, they turned and fled.

"Scum!" Edward Winslow said. "You treated them too gently, William. I'd have cracked their skulls."

Bradford silently fingered the staff as they resumed their walk. "No, Edward, they aren't scum. They had no intention of robbing us, you see. They're decent, honorable men who are afraid. Their fear confused them."

Winslow looked at him blankly.

Bradford did not speak again until they emerged from the alley and made their way past rows of solidly built stone houses. "The Dutch government has been very kind to us, and so have the clergy. But some of the people see us taking work away from them—"

"We don't! At least, you don't. No one made fustian here until you opened your plant. Now a dozen natives have followed your example. So there's more work, not less."

"Men who are afraid they're losing employment, afraid they and their families will starve, rarely think logically and reasonably." Bradford turned the staff over in his hands, then suddenly threw it into a snowbank. "They wanted to frighten me, perhaps 'teach me a lesson,' as they might put it."

"But what did they hope to gain?" Winslow persisted.

"At best, they thought I'd dismiss my workmen and hire them. At worst, they intended to give me a beating for daring not to hire them in the first place. This experience is not unusual."

"True," Winslow frowned. "John Carver received an anonymous, threatening letter two weeks ago, and it was just last month that a crowd gathered outside Isaac Allerton's tailor shop to jeer."

Bradford's sigh was more eloquent than words.

"We don't belong in Holland, William."

"I'd put it the other way round. I believe that many of us have adjusted to the Dutch way of life. But there are some people here who will never accept us. To them, we'll always be foreigners."

"I don't mind admitting that I feel like an alien," Winslow said bitterly.

They walked the rest of the distance in gloomy silence, each busy with his own thoughts. Mary Brewster admitted them to the modest house, and the men smiled at two of her small sons, who were playing in the tiny vestibule.

One of the boys looked up at the guests, giggled and said, "*Het is tijd om naar bed ta gaan.*"

William Brewster appeared in the archway that separated the hall from the small parlor. Ordinarily he was one of the most mild-mannered of men, but he scowled at his son and said sharply, "How often must I tell you to speak English under this roof?"

The child clapped a hand over his mouth, and his mother came to his defense. "He was merely saying it's time to go to bed."

"So it is, but he isn't out somewhere playing with his Dutch friends now. He's English, and he mustn't forget it!" Controlling himself, Brewster welcomed the new arrivals and led them into the parlor.

Eight or nine men, members of the informal council that governed the Separatist community in Leyden, were gathered there, listening to Pastor Robinson. "Our affairs become more critical with each passing month," the clergyman declared. "Most of the adults in our congregation are hampered by their inability to speak the Dutch language—"

"Our boys and girls speak it all too fluently," Brewster interrupted.

"Precisely," Robinson said vigorously. "Our men can't earn enough to support their families, so their elder children must go to work instead of staying in school to finish their education."

John Carver nodded sympathetically. He did not share the problems of the others, for he and his wife had no children, and his investments had made him relatively wealthy. So his sense of detachment made it easier for him to see the situation clearly. "You make the same complaints at meeting after meeting, my friends. It's time to think of a remedy."

Brewster stood. "That's what I've done, and that's why I asked all of you here tonight. Will you come with me?"

He led them to the cellar, where several candle stubs were lighted. In their flickering glare the men saw a small hand-operated printing press, several neatly partitioned boxes of metal type, some jars of ink and a roller.

"Here," their host told them, "you see the Pilgrim Press." He picked up a long sheet of paper, on which something was printed, and thrust it into Bradford's hands. "Read this, William."

Bradford held the paper close to the nearest candle and began to read aloud. "*Fellow Englishmen: how long will you meekly tolerate religious injustice? Strike off your bonds and take a stand for the freedom of worship that is your true English heritage.*" He broke off suddenly, horrified.

The others were gaping at him.

"Are you intending to send this — this treasonable document to England?" he demanded hoarsely.

"Two thousand copies went off last week to a trusted friend in London, who'll distribute them. I'd rather not identify him — even to any of you — as he's placing his life in jeopardy for our cause. And as I've been working every night to print still more, I hope to have another two thousand by the end of the month."

Hard-headed Isaac Allerton muttered to Bradford and Winslow, "I think he's gone mad."

Brewster heard him and smiled. "I hope to convince you otherwise, Isaac. Shall we go upstairs? I think we'll be more comfortable there."

They trooped up to the parlor again in a tense atmosphere. Bradford could not curb his impatience, however, and did not wait for an explanation. "You'll win few converts to our faith with these tactics. What you will do is outrage King James, and our brethren in England will be made to suffer even more severely for their beliefs!"

Robinson rebuked him with a frown. "Our brothers at home are already persecuted. We've embarked on this venture in the full knowledge of what we're doing," Bradford said.

"We agree," the clergyman said, "that we find life in Holland unsatisfactory. Although no one interferes with our worship, most of us live in dire need of adequate food and clothing and shelter."

"Pastor Robinson and I have been worrying about our plight for a long time," Brewster added. "Earlier this year we made a great decision. The Pilgrim Press plays a role in our plan. Now that we've put it into operation, the time has come to take you into our confidence and win your approval."

"Without you we can do nothing," Robinson declared. Leaning forward in his chair, he lowered his voice so the Brewster children could not hear him from their bedrooms directly above the parlor. "I don't regret having come to Holland. I hope you feel as I do."

There was a murmur of agreement, and Bradford said, "At the time we had no choice."

"A great deal has happened in ten years," Robinson said. "Circumstances have changed, and I believe the day is soon approaching when we must move again."

Sam Fuller, a slow-spoken young man, shrugged helplessly. "France and Spain are the ancient enemies of England, and wouldn't allow us to pass their borders. The princes of the Italian and German states think we're troublemakers. Every door in Europe is closed to us."

"In *Europe*," the clergyman repeated.

Brewster rose to his feet. "We propose," he said, emphasizing each word, "to establish a permanent community of our own, where we will be our own masters."

"Where?" Bradford asked brusquely.

"With God's help — and your endorsement — we will settle in the New World."

In the stunned moment that followed, someone gasped. Then it was so quiet that the clock on the mantel above the hearth seemed to tick loudly.

"I have been reading the books published by Captain John Smith," Robinson told the startled members of the council. "A few of you may be familiar with his work. It was he who founded a place called Jamestown in Sir Walter Raleigh's colony of Virginia."

"I've read Smith's book about Jamestown," Bradford said. "He went there in 1607, the same year we came here to Leyden."

"Smith has made other voyages along the coast of the New World, too," the clergyman continued. "Farther to the north he explored portions of a land he calls New England, and fish are so plentiful off a portion of the shore there that he has named the place Cape Cod. The climate in Virginia is warmer, so it seems more sensible for us to go there."

Allerton gestured impatiently. "With no dishonor meant to you or Master Brewster, Pastor, you're both daydreaming. Most of us thank the Almighty when we have enough coppers in our purses to buy bread for our families. An expedition to the New World would cost a great fortune. We'd have to buy huge ships, mountains of supplies, tons of equipment!"

"Financing such a venture would be virtually impossible," Bradford declared, annoyed at the lack of realism shown by the older men. "But it would be even more difficult to get something far more precious — a royal charter. The Crown claims all of the New World discovered by Englishmen, and no colonies may be set up there without King James' permission." He laughed savagely. "Can you imagine him granting such a right to us, to Separatists whom he considers traitors?"

Robinson and Brewster waited for him to subside. "The Pilgrim Press will help us to obtain the right to settle in the New World," the clergyman said.

Bradford and Allerton exchanged long looks of disbelief.

"You see, my friends," Brewster explained gently, "the King thought he was rid of us when we went into exile. But our brethren have remained a thorn in his flesh that he can't pluck out. Now the tracts that I write and publish will stir up all of England."

"There are a few highly placed nobles friendly to our cause," Robinson went on. "I've been corresponding with them, secretly of course. They assure me that James is heartily sick of Separatists, and will become sicker still, because the pamphlets we publish are being sent to England deliberately in order to goad him. He'll soon realize he can't silence us. We're not allowed to set foot in England, but we continue to defy his authority, to make trouble for him."

"Therefore," Brewster declared triumphantly, "we believe that, in another year at the most, the King will be delighted to grant us permission to settle in the New World. He'll be rid of us permanently, and our brethren in England will want to go with us. The Separatist hornets will vanish from the British Isles, and James will be free of their sting."

"Gentlemen who know the Kling's mind assure me he'll be eager to grant us a charter after our publications have flooded his realm," Robinson said solemnly. "And it may even be that we'll persuade others to think as we do. We'll need a great many recruits if we're to create our own community in the wilderness of the New World."

Bradford tugged absently at the hem of his black woolen doublet as he pondered. He was forced to admit that he could find no flaw in the reasoning of Robinson and Brewster, and felt ashamed of his outburst. "I suppose," he said contritely, "that you've found some way to get the money for this venture?"

The clergyman's smile was forgiving. "England has changed since we left her shores. I'm told in every letter I receive that great crowds gather at the Thames docks in London to watch merchant ships unload tobacco and lumber and furs from Jamestown. Books by Captain Smith and other explorers are bought as fast as they're published. Visitors from the West Indian Islands and other New World settlements are honored guests at the King's court. England is consumed by a fever of curiosity about North America."

Bradford failed to see how that interest could be converted into solid financial support for an extraordinarily expensive undertaking.

Robinson knew what was going through his mind. "There may be gold in Virginia and New England, as there is in the Spanish colonies. But there are other goods as valuable. The Jamestown experiment has proved it, and so have the tropical plantations in Jamaica. There are many men of great wealth who are willing, even anxious, to invest funds in a new colony. I've been provided with lists of eager landowners, great merchants, powerful lords, and it grows longer with every letter I receive."

"There's no lack of adventurous young men," Brewster added, "but the men of wealth do not want to place their funds in the hands of those who might prove irresponsible. They prefer to invest in companies that will sponsor permanent settlements."

"I see." Bradford understood now. "Obviously there aren't many families willing to risk possible dangers and discomforts. That places us in a unique position. We can offer investors permanent financial security. If we should go to the New World, we'd stay there." A sudden feeling of excitement caused his temples to throb. "It may be that our destiny lies in the New World rather than in Holland!"

His wonder and elation were contagious. A farfetched idea — a scheme so wild and daring that no Separatist would have considered it feasible when the refugees had first gone into exile — loomed now as a bright hope.

It was late and bitterly cold when Bradford returned home from the meeting at Brewster's house. His boots squeaked on the hard-packed snow, and his fingers, nose and ears were numb, but he was so happy that he was scarcely aware of the weather. His house was dark, and he let himself in quietly, bolted the front door and silently mounted the steps to the master bedchamber on the second floor.

A cheerful coal fire in the hearth warded off the chill, and he could see by its faint glow that Dorothy was curled up in the huge four-poster bed that dominated the room. He thought she was asleep, but she sat up as he stood before the fire warming his hands.

"I was afraid something terrible happened to you," she said. "You're very late."

Bradford decided to say nothing about the attempted attack by the journeyman weaver and his friends. Violence of any sort worried her, and it would be useless to tell her that, as the assault had failed, there was no cause for concern. "Our meeting tonight was the most important we've ever held." He wanted to share the good news with her. "We want to migrate to the New World."

Dorothy's eyes widened, a hand crept to her throat, and she made an unsuccessful attempt to speak.

"We hope to establish our own town there. We'll live according to our own standards and worship as we please."

She moaned, fell back on the bed and buried her face in the pillows.

Her reaction dismayed him. Trying to be fair, he reminded himself that she had spent more than half of her life in Holland. Having grown to womanhood in an alien land, she could not appreciate the opportunity that beckoned.

"I'd die there," Dorothy muttered, "and so would the baby."

It was difficult for Bradford to curb his annoyance. "Nonsense," he said. "From all we've read and heard, it's a land of plenty."

"It's a savage wasteland!" she cried, tears streaming down her cheeks. "There are no cities, no roads. How would we live?"

"You forget," he said dryly, losing patience, "that I was a farmer before I went into exile."

She closed her eyes, and the tears ran down into the collar of her thick, flannel nightgown. "I'd never see Mama and Papa again."

"They'd come, too."

"They're too sensible!" she retorted. "They'll stay in Amsterdam for the rest of their lives."

He imagined she was probably right. Some of the older Separatists would be reluctant to make another major move. But it was essential for the welfare of the whole group that the younger people go. "Regardless of what they might do," he said, his voice becoming sharp, "we'll migrate. We owe it to ourselves and our child."

"I refuse to let my baby leave Holland." Dorothy was becoming hysterical. "I suppose you can force me to go with you — and to die — but I refuse to take John!"

He made a last attempt to placate her. "You know nothing about the New World. Tomorrow I'll give you one of Captain Smith's books to read. You'll learn that the soil is rich, the forests are filled with game, and there are vast oceans of trees waiting to be cut down to make snug homes."

She saw he had made up his mind, but made a desperate attempt to persuade him to change it. "Please, William, don't let others influence you. We have everything we want and need right here. You own a successful business, our house is lovely—"

"My conscience won't let me live in comfort when my brethren are starving," he said harshly. "For better or worse, I've committed us to make the journey to America!"

4

By 1619 the plight of the Separatists had become desperate. Life in Holland was increasingly difficult. Work was still scarce, and the Dutch authorities had become less friendly to the refugees, with good reason. The British ambassador had delivered a blistering protest to the government because of the activities of the Pilgrim Press, which had published scores of pamphlets and smuggled them across the English Channel.

Those pamphlets had borne fruit, however. King James had let it be known that, although he would not grant the Separatists a charter to establish a colony in the New World, he would be delighted to be rid of them. Therefore he would let them set up a colony on British-owned soil in the New World without going through the formality of obtaining a charter.

The Pilgrims themselves would have been satisfied with such an arrangement, but the potential investors were not. These wealthy men felt they would have too little protection. So two Separatist elders, John Carver and Robert Cushman, were sent to London for the purpose of negotiating with the Crown. To the surprise of everyone, they persuaded James to grant the charter.

In the meantime, members of the church in Holland had decided it was wiser not to settle in Virginia, for the Church of England was already the official state religion in Jamestown. Instead, they thought, they would go to New England. Again the wealthy merchants and landowners balked. Virtually nothing was known of that wilderness, they said. There would be no protection for their investment, and they refused to part with their money.

Carver and Cushman could not persuade them to change their minds. The Pilgrim leaders realized that drastic action of some sort was necessary if they hoped to salvage their plan, and an emergency meeting was held. Representatives of both the Leyden and Amsterdam groups met behind closed doors at Pastor Robinson's house. William Brewster, who now held the title of "Ruling Elder," or president of the congregation, remained behind after the others had gone; and although he had arrived at Robinson's house early in the morning, he did not leave until very late in the afternoon.

Dusk was falling when he finally returned to his own home, and his worried wife was waiting for him at the door. She was relieved to see him, but asked no questions, knowing he would tell her whatever he thought appropriate. "Two of your pupils came here this afternoon, but I told them not to wait," she said.

"I'm afraid I won't be able to give any more tutoring lessons in English to Dutch students," Brewster replied.

They had no other source of income, and Mary Brewster became alarmed. "How will we live?"

He made no reply until he had led her to their bedroom and closed the door. "You and the children will be supported by church funds that Pastor Robinson will give you."

She braced herself. "What will you do?"

"I'm being sent to England."

Mary sank into a chair, covering her face with her hands. "The Crown knows you're the publisher of the Pilgrim Press. If you're caught, they'll hang you!"

"I must take the risk."

"Why?" she demanded, clutching the arm of her chair so hard that her knuckles turned white.

"Someone in a position of ultimate authority must take charge of the negotiations with the merchants and landowners. There are only two of us who can speak for our entire membership, who can bargain. And Pastor Robinson is needed here."

"No, William! You can't, you mustn't!"

"Ssh. Don't let the children hear you. I don't want them — or anyone else — to know of my mission. My safety depends on secrecy, just as the whole future of our brethren will be settled by the success or failure of my talks."

Mary began to weep. "They have no right to demand that you take such a terrible chance."

"No one asked me to accept this assignment. I volunteered." He patted her shoulder awkwardly. "You see, the merchants have been making greater and greater demands ever since they heard we want to settle in New England rather than Virginia. Some of them have even been insisting that we spend all of our working hours in their service for our first ten years in the New World."

"But that isn't fair." Mary protested.

"Of course it isn't. Carver and Cushman have had to write us for fresh instructions every time the investors change their terms. The merchants have been trying to take advantage of them. But I'll have the power to make the best deal I can get." Brewster went to a chest of drawers and started to remove clean shirts and stockings, which he placed on the bed. "I'm leaving tonight. We've hired the captain of a fishing boat to sail me across the English Channel at dawn."

Mary was aghast. "So soon?"

"Every day is precious. The merchants will lose their enthusiasm if the negotiations drag out too long." He hesitated, then decided to speak frankly. "And I want to get as much done as possible before the King's bailiffs discover that I'm in England. Eventually they'll hear rumors, so I want to act quickly."

"Eventually," she replied dispiritedly, her shoulders drooping, "they'll search for you — and find you. Then they'll drag you off to prison, and the King will order you hanged in a public ceremony. I beg you, dear, think of the children and me before you do this wild, reckless thing!"

"It's because of my family, and the families of all the others in the congregation, that I'm willing to risk capture and death. Many of our people will starve if we stay much longer in Holland, and the children will become Dutch in every way. We can't go home to England without giving up our church and our beliefs. We have no choice, Mary."

"Do your duty," she told him and, reaching up, kissed him.

Her acceptance of his decision relieved Brewster. Now he could concentrate all of his energies on his dangerous mission. He knew the odds against him were high, but could not allow himself to contemplate the possibility of failure. The right of men to worship as they pleased depended on his ability to obtain reasonable terms from investors while evading King James' law enforcement officers.

The fishing schooner *De Hemel* spent two days and two nights in a ceaseless struggle with mountainous waves and strong winds in the North Sea but eventually gained the sanctuary of England's Thames River. The last stage of her voyage to London was uneventful. Brewster remained below deck as the ship made her way slowly through familiar countryside, and although he was eager to see the land from which he had been exiled for twelve long years he resisted the temptation.

Not until the master of the vessel had docked at a wharf only a stone's throw from the grim, massive Tower of London did the fugitive dare to emerge into the open. The night was dark, but he was able to make out the heavy stone walls of the Tower, and stared at them in silence. If he should be captured, he would be cast into a cell in the castle that was now used exclusively to house famous or notorious prisoners, and probably would die on a gallows in the Tower courtyard.

Steeling himself, Brewster picked up his traveling box, slung it over one shoulder and held it securely with a strap which he wound around his left hand. Then he shook hands with the captain, who wished him good luck, and stepped onto the wharf.

The stars were hidden behind banks of clouds, and a raw wind was blowing as Brewster walked through dark streets in the direction of the Strand, a main thoroughfare that cut through a workers' district only a short distance from King James' palace at Whitehall. It was odd to hear passing pedestrians speaking English rather than Dutch, and Brewster warned himself not to ask directions of strangers. He still spoke in the strong, distinctive accents of Yorkshire, and anyone who heard him would know he was not a Londoner. When the authorities heard he was in the city, as they would after he started meeting with prospective investors, they would hunt for a Yorkshireman. He might be inconspicuous in appearance, but his accent would give him away.

Two members of the watch, the local police force, sauntered down the cobbled street toward him, and Brewster pulled his broad-brimmed hat lower over his eyes. He felt an urge to flee into an alley, but curbed the impulse. Instead he forced himself to continue walking at the same even pace.

Both officers carried long staffs with lead-weighted ends, and one was swinging a lantern. Brewster was sorry he was carrying a traveling box, for it called attention to him. He would have been wiser to stuff his belongings into an old sack, but it was too late now to wish he had planned more carefully.

The watchman raised his lantern, and both officers peered at the man who was no more than four or five feet from them.

Brewster caught his breath, but his face remained impassive. Unless customs had changed radically in the years he had been away, respectable citizens paid no attention to the officers of the watch. He could feel the men studying him, and knew his traveling box had attracted their notice. But he reminded himself that, as yet, he had no real cause to be afraid. Literally no one knew he was in England.

The watchmen lost interest in him. His woolen suit was old but clean, and his lined face was that of an honest man.

The lantern disappeared down the street, and Brewster, wiping a film of perspiration from his forehead, realized he was trembling.

Unable to control his impatience now, he walked more rapidly to a narrow side street that twisted down toward the Thames River. He went to the door of a tiny wooden house badly in need of paint and, still holding his box over his shoulder, rapped quietly.

After what seemed like a long wait the door creaked open, and an attractive young woman with blonde hair and an erect bearing stood in the frame. "What do you want?" she demanded, then peered at him more closely and gasped. "Elder Bre—"

"Don't mention my name," he said hurriedly.

She caught his arm, pulled him into the house and bolted the door. Too stunned to speak, she could only stare at him in the flickering light cast by a candle set in a wall socket.

Alice Carpenter Southworth had been a young girl the last time Brewster saw her. She was a woman now, and lovelier than ever, but he would have known her anywhere. "I'm sorry I startled you," he said, "but I had no time to send you advance word that I was coming. Besides, it wouldn't have been safe."

Alice hugged her parents' oldest and best friend, then led him to the cramped living room, where Edward Southworth, her husband, blinked in astonishment and grew pale when he recognized the visitor. Brewster quickly explained his mission to the loyal young Separatist couple.

"You'll stay here with us," Alice said. "I'll hide you in our attic."

"Thank you," Brewster replied. "I've been hoping I could find shelter here. You wrote to Pastor Robinson that you'd do anything for our cause, and I'm taking you at your word. But I don't want to place you or your children in danger."

Alice waved aside the possibility that she or her family might suffer. She would bring him his meals in the attic, she said, and he would leave his sanctuary only at night, when the children were asleep and neighbors, who might ask questions, would be less inclined to notice that there was a stranger in the house.

Southworth, a weak but amiable man, agreed with everything his wife said, and went off at once to tell John Carver and Robert Cushman of his arrival. A meeting with the investors was to be arranged for the following evening, if possible. Cushman and Carver were instructed to tell them that someone had come from Holland to take charge of the negotiations. But, Brewster emphasized, they were not to be told his identity.

Rumors would start to fly soon enough, he knew. When King James and his ministers heard that a middle-aged Separatist had come from Holland to conduct the talks, it wouldn't be difficult for them to guess that the negotiator was the publisher of the Pilgrim Press. Then dozens of bailiffs and hundreds of soldiers would search for him, and if he should be caught, there was little doubt he would be condemned to death as a traitor.

Brewster could only hope and pray he would succeed in his mission before the almost inevitable day when he would be captured and made a prisoner of the Crown.

Twenty men were gathered in the library on the second floor of the comfortable house near London Bridge. The host, James Sherley, a prosperous goldsmith, made certain his guests were plentifully supplied with ham and veal pies, oyster puddings and whole, roasted chickens. Servants circulated unobtrusively, filling goblets with wine, and a sideboard table was laden with delicacies. Everyone was weary, for meetings had been held almost every evening for six weeks to hammer out an agreement between the Separatists and their wealthy financial supporters.

But tonight a holiday atmosphere prevailed, the men were in a happy mood, and huge quantities of food and wine disappeared. Two of the Separatist representatives, Carver and Cushman, ate hungrily, but William Brewster had no appetite. The long weeks of negotiations, the constant maneuvering to obtain better terms, had tired him. And the tension caused by his fear of recognition added to the strain.

He sat patiently, silently, at a table on which a score of documents were spread. Somber in black, he did not join in the gaiety as he waited for the signing of the contracts that would make the agreement official. Sherley, who was the secretary-treasurer of the investors' group, finally joined him and held up a hand for silence.

"Gentlemen," he said, "this is an historic occasion. We have agreed to provide funds for the establishment of a colony in the land called New England. Our gold will be used to charter ships and buy supplies of all kinds. The colonists will be members of the Separatist church and other persons whom they can persuade to accompany them across the ocean. Am I correct, Master X?" He turned jovially to Brewster, who had been known by no other name during the talks.

"I'd like to emphasize two points," Brewster declared, rising to his feet. "In the years to come, you who are investing in our venture will continue to supply us with funds. We will repay you with furs and lumber of the highest quality."

"We want gold and diamonds!" a wealthy merchant shouted.

"You shall have all that we find," Brewster replied with a faint smile. "Rest assured, gentlemen, that as our colony grows larger, year by year, your return on your investment will increase."

Sherley picked up a quill pen, dipped it in a jar of ink and signed each copy of the contract. Then he handed the pen to Brewster, who immediately beckoned to John Carver.

"No, Master X," Sherley said firmly. "You've been the spokesman for the Separatists. We must have your signature, not that of an assistant."

His point was valid, and Brewster realized he could conceal his identity no longer. Taking the pen, he started to sign the copies.

Sherley seized one, glanced at it and then announced, "William Brewster!"

A hush fell over the assemblage. Most of the financiers were members of the Church of England, loyal followers of King James, and without exception they had heard of the notorious gadfly whose pamphlets had dared to mock the authority and dignity of the Crown.

The secret was out, and Brewster unflinchingly returned the stares of nobles, landowners and merchants. Perhaps some had guessed his identity, but had kept their thoughts to themselves, knowing everything would be ruined if they revealed their suspicions prematurely. Now they no longer had a choice. No matter what they might think of Brewster, regardless of whether they liked him, it was their duty, as honorable subjects of the King, to tell James that the traitor had come to England.

Hastily signing the last copies, Brewster walked to the door. "I don't want to spoil your party, gentlemen," he said calmly. "But I must leave London tonight, for obvious reasons." Carver and Cushman, who looked alarmed, would have joined him, but he waved them back into the library.

Taking his hat and cloak from a servant, he slipped out into the night. He started off toward the Southworth house and, after making certain he was not being followed, increased his pace.

The gibbet seemed very near, and Brewster shivered. But he was not downhearted, for no matter what might happen to him, the contracts had been signed and the cruel dilemma of the Separatists had been solved. Even if he should be caught and hanged, other members of the congregation would start life anew in America.

A heavy pounding on the front door of the dilapidated house off the Strand awakened Brewster, who had dropped off to sleep fully dressed. A quick glance out of the small window at the end of the attic told him it was morning. Slipping into his boots, he crouched close to the thin floorboards in order to hear what was happening below. His few belongings had already been removed from the attic. His traveling box now reposed in the cellar, where it innocently held some of Alice's linen, and his clothing was resting in Edward's chest of drawers. None of the items could be identified.

"Open in the King's name!" a man called in a deep voice.

Alice took her time responding to the command. "We're decent, law-abiding citizens," she said in mock indignation as she finally unbolted and opened the door. "What do you want here?"

"We carry a search warrant bearing the royal seal. We're looking for a traitor named William Brewster."

"Master William Brewster is in Holland!" Alice spoke loudly and distinctly, hoping the fugitive in the attic would hear her.

Brewster grinned appreciatively.

"We have reason to believe otherwise. Will you stand aside, or must we use force?"

"I have nothing to hide," Alice replied. "I'll even take you through the house myself."

Brewster had heard enough. He knew Alice would use delaying tactics, but he needed every precious second. Jumping to his feet, he rolled up the pallet on which he had slept, threw it into a corner and made a final check of the bare attic to reassure himself that no tell-tale piece of personal property was left behind.

Men were thumping on the floorboards below, and Brewster crept to the window, opened it and pulled himself up onto the ledge. The frame was barely wide enough for him to squeeze through it, and he scraped the back of his left hand on the weather-roughened wood of the shutter. But he could not take time to attend to his injury. Balancing precariously on the ledge, he carefully closed the shutter.

Three mounted cavalrymen in plumed helmets and short scarlet capes were guarding the entrance to the house, he saw, and were holding the horses of the others who were conducting the search, if one of them happened to look up, all would be lost.

Whispering a prayer, Brewster reached for the drainpipe of iron that extended from the lip of the roof gutter to the street. A light rain had fallen before dawn, making the pipe slippery, but he grasped it with all his might, swung away from the ledge and curled his legs around the pipe. He felt it tremble, and was afraid it might break away from the outer wall. If that happened, he would be catapulted to certain death below, but the pipe strained against the thin half-hoops attached to the wall and held firm.

Clutching the pipe with a strength born of desperation, Brewster pulled himself up, hand over hand, toward the relative safety of the flat roof. Neighbors on the opposite side of the street certainly would see him if they glanced out of their windows, he knew, but he could not let himself think of anything except his own immediate task.

His arms and shoulders ached, and it was agony to haul himself toward the roof. Twice he slipped, almost losing his balance, and clung to the pipe. He gasped for breath, but did not dare pause to rest, and continued to pull himself up, inch by tortured inch.

Suddenly, to his horror, he saw a handkerchief fall from the hip pocket of his breeches and flutter toward the ground. There was nothing he could do to retrieve it, and he watched in fascinated horror as it floated toward the head of one of the troopers. Then a small puff of a gentle breeze caused the handkerchief to change direction slightly, and it landed no more than a foot behind the soldier's mount. Perhaps the gelding sensed that something out of the ordinary had happened, for it shifted its position. A heavy hoof landed on the handkerchief, grinding it into the wet, dirty cobblestones.

The feeling of relief that flooded Brewster made him dizzy, but he was not yet safe, and continued to climb until, at last, he was able to hoist himself onto the roof. He drew back from the gutter, lay down and pressed against the wet blocks of soot-smeared wood.

Panting, utterly exhausted, he wanted to weep, but was heartened by the realization that he had accomplished a remarkable physical feat — all the more astonishing because it had been performed by a man fifty-three years old who had engaged in no violent physical exercise since his youth.

A column of black smoke rose from the chimney of the house next door, and Brewster realized that breakfast was being cooked there over a coal fire. The smoke drifted toward him, causing him to cough, and he bit his forefinger to prevent himself from suffering a spasm that the troops in the street would hear. For the better part of an hour the smoke swept over him, inflaming his eyes and making his throat so raw that it was torture to swallow. But he had no complaint, and when he heard hoofbeats in the street, he crawled to the edge of the roof and peered down cautiously.

The troops were departing, and he knew that, barring an unexpected emergency, he was safe.

He did not dare risk crawling down the drainpipe in broad daylight, and remained on the roof all day. He was chilled and ravenously hungry when, soon after nightfall, Alice called to him softly from the attic window and threw one end of a rope to him.

He tied it around his waist and painfully lowered himself down the drainpipe.

The Southworths helped him climb into the attic, and Alice embraced him. "I couldn't imagine where you'd gone," she said, "until I saw your footprint on the outer window ledge. I thank the Almighty that the troops didn't notice it."

Brewster enjoyed the luxury of standing erect and stretching. "I've placed you young people in enough jeopardy," he said. "I must leave as soon as it becomes safe for me to travel."

"You'll do no such thing," Alice told him. "There's no safer place for you in all England than this house. The captain who was in charge of the search inspected everything, even the inside of my onion bin. He was satisfied you weren't here, and even apologized for any inconvenience he may have caused me."

"I learned today," her husband added, "that the Royal Navy has been ordered to search every ship that sails from the country. And it's said troops are hunting for you in every port."

"So you'll stay right here until the time comes to make the great voyage to the New World," Alice declared.

5

Unexpected complications delayed the departure of the Separatists for the New World in the final months of 1619 and the first half of 1620. The greatest problem was finding suitable shipping. Owners of vessels were reluctant to risk losing their property in uncharted seas. Ships' officers and crews had little desire to cross an ocean thousands of miles wide, and the prospect of landing in the wilderness of a virtually unknown destination was bleak.

Eventually, however, two ships were chartered. They were the *Mayflower*, a sturdy vessel of one hundred and eighty tons, and the *Speedwell*, a small craft of only sixty tons. Preparations for the voyage were hurried. Cushman and Carver, who had remained in England, were kept busy buying supplies and provisions of all kinds.

The Separatists in Holland were forced to make a painful decision. Space on the ships was limited; the two ships could accommodate no more than about one hundred and sixty passengers. The financiers in London had recruited a number of nonchurch members as colonists, as they were anxious that the company should include men who possessed special, necessary skills. This reduced the available space still more, so only a small fraction of the Leyden congregation was able to make the voyage.

Pastor Robinson decided to remain behind with the majority of his flock, most of whom preferred to sail later. William Bradford and his wife were members of the company that left Holland on the *Speedwell*, but Dorothy became so hysterical at the thought of taking their five-year-old son with them that Bradford reluctantly left the child in Holland with her parents.

The *Mayflower* was waiting for the smaller ship at Southampton, one of the busiest English ports. There, as final preparations were made for the long voyage, the Separatists met the nonchurch members who would become their neighbors, associates and friends. Among them were Captain Miles Standish, a former army officer, who had been engaged as the colony's military leader, and Stephen Hopkins, who had accompanied John Smith on one of his voyages of discovery and was the only person in the entire group who had ever visited the New World. There was also a husky young carpenter, John Alden, who had been hired to supervise the building of the settlers' homes and other structures.

The Southampton wharves were a magnet that drew hundreds of curious citizens to the waterfront. A company of soldiers was on hand to make certain that none of the despised Separatists changed their minds and remained in England. Church members were not allowed to wander through the town, but were forced to remain in the dock area. They were exiles, and the Crown did not intend to let them forget it.

Sellers of food and clothing, hardware and firearms did a brisk trade as the future colonists made their last purchases before leaving the civilized world. So many peddlers displayed their wares that few noticed one old man with white hair and a beard. Bradford and Winslow invited him on board the *Mayflower* to inspect his merchandise and, when they were alone with him in the passengers' quarters, carefully bolted the outer door.

Then William Brewster emerged from his disguise, brushing powder from his hair and removing his false beard. There was still a high price on his head, so he stayed in hiding on board the ship. His wife and several of his children joined him there, and he did not set foot on land again. His friends hid him so successfully, in fact, that not even Captain Christopher Jones, the *Mayflower*'s master, knew he was on the ship.

The *Speedwell* had proved unseaworthy on the trip across the North Sea and English Channel from Holland, and several weeks were lost while she was fitted with a new mainmast and other repairs were made. At last all was ready, and on August 5, 1620, the two ships sailed out of Southampton harbor, with the *Mayflower* in the lead. The Pilgrims, as all of the colonists now called themselves, were excited but were doomed to disappointment.

The balky *Speedwell* reacted erratically and developed a bad leak. So the ships put into the port of Dartmouth to make further repairs. In all, the expedition put to sea three times, and on each occasion was forced to turn back. Captain Jones was worried, for the summer was slipping away, and the storms of the approaching autumn would make a voyage hazardous.

Frantic attempts were made to repair the *Speedwell*, but the labor was in vain. Finally it was decided to leave her behind, and many of her passengers were transferred to the *Mayflower*, their provisions, supplies and other goods being stored in her cramped hold. Captain Jones called a halt when the passenger list soared to one hundred and two persons. He could accommodate no more, and some of the *Speedwell* group, bitterly disappointed, were forced to return to Holland and await a later opportunity to join their friends in the New World.

At long last, after almost interminable delays, the *Mayflower* sailed alone out of Plymouth harbor on September 6, 1620.

When Captain Jones assured John Carver, the elected leader of the colonists, that they were truly on their way, William

Brewster emerged from hiding. Everyone was delighted to see him, and in the absence of Pastor Robinson he immediately assumed the position of temporary head of the church.

Life on board the crowded ship was difficult. The passengers had one large stove, but were forbidden to use it except in fine weather, as Captain Jones was afraid they might set his ship on fire. So they lived on cold food, principally pickled beef, dried fish and the staple of the sailor's diet, hardtack, which was a dry, brittle biscuit. Water was scarce, and was reserved for the women and children; when the men became thirsty, they had nothing to drink but beer.

The weather was chilly, and as it was impossible to keep the interior of the ship warm, the passengers were cold most of the time. Some discovered they could be comfortable only in their narrow bunks, but Sam Fuller said that people who remained in bed most of the time would become ill. So everyone was compelled to get up for breakfast and exercise as much as possible.

Captain Jones made no secret of his intense dislike for his passengers, whom he considered religious fanatics. He insisted they remain in their own part of the tiny ship. Under no circumstances were they permitted to visit his quarters, and he ordered them not to associate with his crew. He and his men ate hot food cooked on a wood stove in the sailors' galley, but none was offered to the passengers. Even the women and children who were sick had to eat hardtack and preserved meat.

In spite of the restrictions and discomforts, the company was remarkably cheerful. Elder Brewster conducted a worship service every morning, and Edward Winslow conducted classes in reading, spelling and arithmetic for the children.

The women knitted, cared for their children and, when the weather was not too blustery, walked up and down the deck space the passengers were permitted to use. The men and older boys exercised vigorously, no matter what the weather. Captain Jones was petitioned for the right to fish from the stern, and after being badgered by several requests, finally granted the men the privilege.

Of all the company, only Dorothy Bradford complained of her lot.

The *Mayflower* sailed serenely through calm seas through most of September and early October. Then, late one morning, a fierce hurricane blew in from the southwest. The ship shuddered and tossed as huge waves crashed over her bow. Her hull creaked menacingly, and many of the Pilgrims were afraid she would break up in the mountainous seas. They prayed for relief, but the storm became much worse, and the sailors became concerned.

The *Mayflower* seemed like a living, agonized creature as she struggled against the terrible storm. She plunged from the crests of great waves into the deep troughs between them, protesting with every timber when an avalanche of water crashed against her sides. But Captain Jones kept her under control.

For seventy-two hours the Pilgrims remained below decks, huddling behind doors that were tightly closed to keep out water. The air was foul. The confinement rubbed the already raw nerves of the passengers, and on the fourth day of the storm, young John Howland, a Londoner, could stand it no longer.

Afraid he would go mad if he stayed in the cramped cabin any longer, he walked to the door that led into the passageway.

Before anyone could stop him, he dashed out and started up toward the main deck. Bradford and Hopkins followed him, but halted at the ladder Howland was climbing.

"John, come back!" Bradford called.

Howland paid no attention. Pushing open the hatch above his head, he climbed up onto the open deck, breathing deeply as the hatch cover fell back into place. Greenish-black waves, higher than King James' palace at Whitehall, built up suddenly out of the churning surface of the angry sea, then smashed over the ship. One, higher than the others, loomed off the port bow, looking like a solid wall of water.

Some sailors, lashed to masts as they fought to repair broken lines and shredded sails, shouted loud warnings. But their voices were lost in the roar of the wind.

Too late Howland realized his danger. The mammoth wave seemed to tower almost directly over him, and he tried to scurry back to the hatch cover. But he slipped on the wet deck, lost his balance and fell to one knee.

Then the wave crashed, pouring tons of water over the deck. Howland reached out frantically for something to grasp, but the wave swept him overboard.

Bradford and Hopkins heard his terrified scream. Wasting no time, they tied around their waists the ends of a line they found at the bottom of the ladder. Then they hurried up into the open and hauled themselves to the quarterdeck, where Captain Jones, peering through the heavy rain and spray, was trying to catch a glimpse of the drowning man.

"The blasted idiot!" Jones could not control his rage. "He deserves to die!"

Hopkins' previous experience at sea stood him in good stead. "There he is!" He pointed to a spot in the water amidships, off the starboard side.

The others stared in amazement. Several halyards, lines used to raise and lower sails, had come loose, and were trailing in the sea. Howland, it appeared, had managed to catch hold of one of these ropes, and was clutching it with all of his strength.

"Bring a boat hook!" Jones ordered, and one of the sailors hurried below.

The Captain, accompanied by Bradford and Hopkins, fought his way to the railing of the main deck, and all three of them clung to it. Occasionally one or another lost his footing as waves continued to smash over them, but they were safer when they lashed themselves to the sturdy rail.

One moment Howland was completely submerged, then a wave forced him to the surface again. He bobbed crazily, yet managed to keep his frantic hold on the halyard.

It was impossible to determine whether he had already drowned, whether his clutch was that of a dead man.

It felt as though an eternity passed before the sailor, panting for breath, appeared with a boat hook, a twenty-one foot wooden pole with a curved iron end. "Help me," Jones said.

Bradford and Hopkins immediately understood the situation. Neither they nor the Captain could use more than one hand, for each needed to cling to the rail with the other. Jones grasped the pole, Bradford placed a hand behind his, and Hopkins did the same. The *Mayflower* was still rolling and pitching insanely, unpredictably, so it was difficult to pass the point of the hook through Howland's clothes.

The men tried, then tried again, but each time the hook came free. Then, at last, Jones managed to pass it down the victim's back, inside his water-soaked doublet. A single, sharp twist made the hook secure, and all three pulled on the pole, inching it up, little by little, until they had Howland out of the sea. Two sailors, who were standing by, reached down with their free hands and pulled him on to the deck.

"Take him to my quarters!" Jones called hoarsely, and the entire group fought its way toward the stern, stumbling and sliding on the glistening deck as great waves continued to batter the *Mayflower*.

No one realized it, but the rough handling that Howland received was a form of artificial respiration. He was dragged by his arms, then his legs, and each jolt of the ship jarred him, forcing water from his lungs. But his rescuers, intent only on reaching the Captain's cabin, had no idea whether he was dead or alive.

When they reached the cabin, utterly exhausted, they leaned against the bulkhead for a few moments, too weary to speak. Howland, who was sprawled on the deck at their feet, stirred feebly and opened his eyes.

"He's alive!" Stephen Hopkins said in a hoarse voice, scarcely able to believe the evidence before his eyes.

Jones took some brandy from an earthenware jug, poured a small amount into a glass and, kneeling, fed it to the confused Howland, who swallowed, then coughed.

He gathered strength, then looked around in bewilderment, unable to realize all that had happened to him.

Tears came to Bradford's eyes, and he was convinced, more strongly than ever, that the expedition had Divine protection. "Gentlemen," he said, raising his voice to make himself heard above the thunder of the storm, "a miracle has taken place."

John Howland recovered rapidly from his incredible ordeal, which reaffirmed the strong faith of the Separatists. The astonishing incident had another effect, too. Captain Jones was so impressed that, although the storm continued to rage, he sent the passengers a message that raised their spirits: as soon as the weather cleared, he would allow them to use their stove.

A new hurricane roared up toward the northeast from the West Indian Islands before the old one died out, and the sixth day of unceasing stormy weather was the worst the passengers had known. Nearly everyone was ill, and only a few of the stronger men, among them Bradford, Winslow and Hopkins, were able to stay on their feet. Everyone else lay limply under damp blankets, and Dorothy Bradford, moaning incessantly, cursed her husband, the ship and the day she had left Holland.

Late that night an ominously sharp, cracking sound awakened even the soundest sleepers. Many members of the company felt certain the *Mayflower* had struck a huge underwater boulder. Certainly the vessel behaved as though something serious had happened to her and wallowed helplessly in the raging seas.

Candles were lighted, and the passengers gathered in their main cabin, uncertain what to do next. Few were healthy enough to stand erect, Elder Brewster was too ill to lead them in prayer, and they knew they were at the mercy of the elements. They spent the rest of the night together, badly frightened.

Soon after dawn broke in the sullen sky, Captain Jones came down to the passengers' quarters. There were deep rings of fatigue beneath his eyes, and his voice betrayed his exhaustion as he said, "An accident has placed us in great danger."

Dorothy began to weep hysterically, but no one else made a sound.

"A main beam amidships has broken," the Captain continued. "The wood hasn't yet split through all the way, but when it does, the beam will buckle." He shrugged fatalistically.

"When that happens, the ship may come apart. Even if she holds together, I think it likely that we'll have to turn back."

"No," Bradford said, clenching his fists. "We must go on to the New World!"

A tired, cynical smile lighted Jones' weather-beaten face.

Bradford conferred briefly with John Carver, who was stretched out on a pallet, too sick to move.

"Your prayers can't repair a cracked beam, Master Bradford," the Captain said.

"Thanks to our prayers, we carry equipment you may find useful, sir. Among our belongings in the hold is a huge iron screw, a vise. It will hold a beam more than four feet wide, I believe." He glanced at Sam Fuller for corroboration.

Jones removed his dripping hat and wiped his forehead. "Bring me the vise quickly!"

Bradford, hurrying to the stern hold with Fuller, Hopkins and Winslow, understood how the Captain felt. The fact that the Pilgrims had such a vise was either an accident or the intervention of the Almighty, and Bradford preferred the latter explanation. The screw had been used to support the central beam in the ancient house Fuller had owned in Leyden. The building had proved unsafe, so he had removed the vise after moving his family to another building. Then, not knowing what else to do with the huge instrument, he had brought it with him on the voyage.

Right now, if used effectively, it could mean the difference between life and death for everyone on board the *Mayflower*.

The four men burrowed through piles of supplies, found the vise and, using all their strength, dragged it up to the lower deck. There they found Jones and several members of the crew gazing in horror at the huge beam that was the principal support of the upper deck. The wood, once the trunk of a tremendous tree, was about three and one-half feet in diameter. The crack extended from the bottom upward along almost the entire length of the beam, and was already more than eighteen inches deep.

Jones came to life as soon as he saw the iron screw. "You, there," he barked, jabbing a stubby forefinger at the sailors. "Get to work." Then he turned to the Pilgrims. "Help us," he begged.

Working side by side, the colonists and seamen lifted up the vise and clamped it on the beam. Then, while four men held it in place, the others turned the handle of the vise, tightening it.

The race against time became frantic. Bradford discovered he was acting as foreman of the crew turning the handle, and drove them as relentlessly as he drove himself. When the ship lurched, one or another lost his balance but quickly returned to his post. Battered but grim, the men worked in pairs, pulling at the lever until the bit caught and tightened.

Gradually the crack became thinner, but Bradford did not call a halt until it was invisible. The weary sailors thought their work was finished, but the Captain was not satisfied. Wanting to be doubly certain that the beam would not break, he sent two members of his crew to the forward hold for stout timbers. These were wedged between the beam above and the lower deck below, then nailed into place, and at last Jones declared that the damaged beam had been sufficiently reinforced to remain intact through the worst of storms.

"Now," he said to the four Pilgrims, "I must decide whether to sail on to America or return to England."

Bradford was stunned. "You yourself just said the beam is sound now—"

Jones cut his protest short with an abrupt gesture. "I don't know what other damage the storm may have done. Wait for me in my quarters, if you like." Turning on his heel, he went off to make a careful inspection of the *Mayflower*.

Bradford and the others made their way to the master's cabin. Tired after their labors and soaked by spray as they had crossed the open deck, they sat dejectedly, too weary and discouraged to speak. The critical problem that had endangered the lives of everyone on board had been solved, but if Jones elected to go back to England, they were powerless to force him to continue the voyage.

"If I could sail this ship," Bradford muttered, "I'd put him in irons. We can't let anything prevent us from reaching New England!"

The others looked at each other, but made no reply. Bradford, they had learned, was a man of iron will, a man who let nothing stand between him and the goals he believed right.

"It may be," gentle Sam Fuller said at last, "that we aren't meant to establish a colony."

"Nonsense! There would be no reason for all we've suffered if we went back to England — and then to Holland." There was a note of finality in Bradford's voice that ended the discussion.

After a wait that seemed interminable, Captain Jones came into the cabin. Hanging his dripping cloak and hat on a bulkhead peg, he warmed his hands by rubbing them together. "There are several leaks in the hull above the water level, but none below," he told the tense men. "If we don't encounter any more violent storms, I believe we can reach the shores of North America. On the other hand, our food supplies are running low. We sailed at the wrong season, and this voyage is taking longer than it should."

Bradford stiffened. "We'll ride out the present gale, Captain?"

Jones nodded. "I'm sure of that much."

"Then, sir, I must insist that you live up to your contract with us."

There was a gleam of amusement in the Captain's hard eyes. "I wonder if you realize, Master Bradford, that a ship's master is the absolute ruler of his realm. I make my own decisions."

"You were engaged to take us to the New World. Unless this ship founders, I demand — on behalf of our entire company — that you keep your word."

Jones laughed and held out his hand. "I agree to do it! You saved the *Mayflower* for me today, and I'll take you to Cape Cod if I have to row there." He looked at Bradford with respect. "I've had my doubts about your venture, but if the others in your company are men of half your stature, your colony is as good as established."

Early on the morning of November 9, 1620, the men ate their usual cold breakfast, then went up to the open deck while the women cooked porridge for the children and adults who were ill. This was the sixty-fourth day of the long voyage, and everyone was heartily sick of the sea. Smaller storms had struck the *Mayflower* after she had been battered by the hurricanes, and some of the older Pilgrims marveled that the ship was still afloat.

Dorothy Bradford's ceaseless complaints had irritated everyone, but many of the Pilgrims privately echoed her repeated question, "How much longer will this voyage last?"

Her husband refused to speculate, however. He and Christopher Jones had become good friends, and Bradford knew that the Captain was taking full advantage of the wind, crowding on as much sail as he could. Now, walking up and down the narrow deck with Elder Brewster, who held his arm, Bradford remained confident that the future was bright.

"Your health is almost completely recovered," he said, "and Sam Fuller tells me John Carver grows stronger every day, too."

Brewster was reluctant to admit he still felt weak, that he would not become strong again until he felt dry land beneath his feet. Others, he knew, felt precisely as he did. But he realized that, in his position as Presiding Elder of the Separatist church, he could not reveal to anyone that he frequently suffered from a deep sense of depression.

An inarticulate cry escaped from the lips of the lookout, a sailor perched in the crow's nest, high on the mainmast. The Pilgrims on the deck were startled, and stared up at him.

The seaman cupped his hands. "Land ho!" he shouted, and pointed off the starboard bow.

The passengers raced to the rail. Far off on the horizon they saw a thin, dark smudge, a line so narrow they had to squint in order to make it out.

Captain Jones came down from his quarterdeck to join them. He was smiling, and there was deep pride in his voice as he said, "Yonder lies New England. We'll reach her shores tomorrow."

The Pilgrims, enthralled, gazed in wonder at their Promised Land.

6

The last twenty-four hours spent at sea were unusually busy. The women feverishly packed their belongings, not realizing that many more days would pass before they could go ashore permanently. Children raced up and down, laughing. Crew members were eager to go ashore, too, after the long voyage, and Captain Jones had to restrain them from crowding on too much sail.

But three members of the Pilgrim company quietly withdrew to the privacy of Captain Jones' quarters. There William Brewster, aided by William Bradford and Edward Winslow, wrote the remarkable covenant known to posterity as the Mayflower Compact. They worked for several hours, then summoned all of the adult male colonists to a meeting.

Brewster read the document aloud for the benefit of those who were illiterate. The men were required to take a solemn oath swearing to obey its precepts. Foremost among these was that they would join together to form "a civil body politic." No one was allowed to miss the great significance of this clause.

The colony the Pilgrims were founding was ruled and controlled by Separatist church members, yet they deliberately refrained from setting up a religious colony. They, who had suffered so much because of their belief that church and state should be separate, took great care to protect everyone, regardless of his religious convictions.

Bradford explained for the benefit of those who might not understand. "It is right that our first act should be that of separating our government and our church. We hope that all of you will become church members, but we force none to accept our faith. And, no matter what your beliefs, you are citizens of our colony, each enjoying equal rights."

The Compact stated that the colony's citizens, each with one vote, would enact laws and ordinances for the good of the entire community. Everyone pledged that he would obey these acts.

The oath was taken; then John Carver stepped forward to sign the document. Bradford came next, then Winslow and Brewster. The others followed, one by one, and the Mayflower Compact, America's first charter of freedom, became a reality.

Late in the morning of November 11, 1620, after sixty-six days at sea, the *Mayflower* dropped her anchor in Cape Cod's great natural harbor.

There was so much the prospective colonists needed and wanted. On a long-range basis, they had to find the right place to settle permanently. Obviously, they were looking for a site where the soil was rich, trees plentiful and water supplies ample.

For the immediate present, their wants were simpler. They needed fresh water to fill the almost-empty casks on board the ship. They had to have firewood to ward off the biting chill of a New England winter. And they hoped they would find natives — Indians, according to Captain John Smith's account — who would sell them meat and grain and vegetables. Everyone was heartily sick of the pickled beef and fish, the tasteless flour cakes and flat barley bread that had been the staples of the long voyage.

A group of men went ashore, the passengers commanded by Captain Standish, the overall party in charge of the *Mayflower*'s master, Captain Jones. The countryside was bleak, the ground underfoot barren, and a sharp wind from the west numbed the men. John Alden, one of the youngest in the party, could not conceal his disappointment as he blew on his hands to warm them.

"This looks like a desert," he said.

Bradford stamped his feet on the hard-packed sand to restore his circulation. "The surroundings don't bother me," he replied. "I thank God that I can feel the soil of the New World under my feet."

Carver, looked tired and strained after the long voyage, smiled wanly. "We'll need soil blacker than this if we hope to grow crops!"

Jones nervously interrupted them. "Come along," he said impatiently. "I'll be ready to go back to the ship as soon as we've gathered some firewood." He pointed toward a stand of low trees some distance inland.

Standish, who hated to share authority with anyone, beckoned to his own subordinates. "You and your sailors can get the wood, Captain, while we look for a stream or pond." He hoisted a water barrel onto his shoulder, and the other Separatists followed his example.

Jones was alarmed. "I forbid the splitting of our forces! If we're attacked by savages—"

"There's no sign of life anywhere," Standish retorted. "And if you should see Indians, and they attack you, fire a pistol as a warning."

Bradford grinned. "Of course. We'll come running fast enough. And we'll expect you to do the same if we get into difficulties."

The idea was sensible, Jones knew, so he reluctantly agreed.

The colonists moved inland at a rapid pace, Standish in the lead. They marched across sand dunes, seeing no vegetation except a few long, dry wisps of grass that bent low beneath the force of the wind. Then they saw a patch of scrub pines in the distance and headed toward the trees. Standish checked his blunderbuss, making it ready for immediate use, and the others needed no urging to do the same. They had reached the land they hoped to make their home, but had to be ready for danger. If they were disappointed because the area was so empty, so inhospitable, they kept their thoughts to themselves.

They spread out after they reached the forest and walked slowly, cautiously over a carpet of snow, dead branches and thick, brown leaves. There was no sound but the crackling of wood beneath their feet as they pushed farther inland. It was apparent to everyone that this part of Cape Cod was uninhabited, for they saw no sign of wildlife in the woods, no plants that might produce edible food in the summer. They could only hope that, in days to come, they would find some other spot where it might be possible to found their colony.

The firm voice of young Edward Winslow, who was on the far left flank, broke the silence. "Captain Standish!" he shouted. "There's a little river here!"

The whole party hurried toward the left, and everyone stared at a small, swift-flowing stream moving beneath an inch-thick crust of ice.

"That water," John Carver said huskily, "is a symbol of hope."

Bradford agreed, and was moved, too. But this was no weather for daydreaming. He took a small axe from his belt and went to work chopping the ice. Others did the same, and Standish cautioned the more enthusiastic not to use the butts of their muskets, as the water could ruin the effectiveness of the weapons.

"Maybe we'll catch some fish," Alden said.

Bradford smiled at the ignorance of a city dweller. "It might be that there are a few trout in the river, but not at this season. They've probably gone out to sea, where it's warmer."

The men worked hard for more than two hours, and when they returned to the *Mayflower*, the entire company gathered around them to taste the fresh, clear water.

Elder Brewster sipped from a mug, a contented expression on his lined face. "I prefer this to the most precious of wines," he said.

Bradford remained silent. The water was important, as was the firewood that blazed in the cookstoves. But he was worried because no food had been found and no natives had appeared. He realized that the entire company would have to live on board the ship until the right site was located. Those who thought that everyone could move ashore as soon as houses could be built would be bitterly disappointed. The New World had been reached, but the band's problems were just beginning.

Forty-eight hours later the weather turned milder, and the women who were in good health were taken ashore, under escort, to wash clothes and bed linen. Huge mounds of laundry were dumped on the ground near the bank of the river. The men chopped away the melting ice, then moved off to stand sentry duty in the forest.

Mary Brewster took charge, and efficiently organized the work party, paying no attention to those who complained that the water was shockingly cold. Soft, semi-liquid soap brought from Holland and England was scrubbed into the clothes, and for want of better implements, the women ponded the garments with stones. Not until much later would they learn they were using the Indian technique of washing.

Some of the older women, members of the Separatist church, began to sing hymns. The younger group, which had gathered on the far bank of the river, was in a lighter mood. Pretty Susanna White, the sister of Deacon Sam Fuller, could not keep from giggling wildly, continuously, and Priscilla Mullins looked at her curiously. "May I know what's so funny?"

Susanna wiped her eyes with the back of a hand, then exploded again as she continued to scrub a shirt. "I thought of myself as a heroine on the voyage. I really did. Every night as I went off to sleep I told myself of the wonderful life that awaited us here. I don't know what I expected when we got here, but I had daydreams of coming ashore to the cheers of a huge crowd."

Priscilla began to laugh, too. "I know what you mean. I doubt if there's a drum or a trumpet in the whole New World, but it would have been so nice to be greeted by a serenading band." She placed one of her father's shirts on a broad, flat stone and began to pound it with a smaller stone. Her laughter became louder. "Oh, dear. Now see what you've done."

Dorothy Bradford looked at her companions in silent, glum contempt.

"Aren't we absurd?" Susanna gasped, and Priscilla nodded cheerfully.

"I think," Dorothy said acidly, "that both of you have lost your wits."

They blinked in astonishment as they glanced at her.

"We're in the midst of a ferocious wilderness," she continued angrily. "There isn't a house anywhere, not a friendly soul to make us welcome. Savages may attack and kill us at any moment. We have nothing to eat except the dreadful, tasteless stores on the *Mayflower*. Here we stand, bending over filthy clothing, working like slaves — and freezing our hands. I see nothing amusing in our situation."

Susanna's laughter died away, and she exchanged a glance with Priscilla before she turned back to Dorothy. "Everything you say is true enough, I suppose — if you want to look at things that way. I don't. I'm too pleased to feel solid ground under my feet again."

"And to know we'll soon be wearing clean clothes," Priscilla added vigorously.

"Don't you see?" Susanna asked. "The voyage is behind us. After all our years of worry, we're here at last."

Priscilla understood perfectly, and her eyes became soft as she said, "Yes, we've come home."

"How dare you call this wilderness home?" Dorothy's voice was shrill, and she didn't realize she was shouting. "Home is where my parents are, in their lovely, comfortable house in Amsterdam. They have enough good food to eat, they're warm and they aren't threatened by savages and wild beasts! That's where I want to be!"

It was strange, Susanna thought, that Dorothy made no mention of the child she had left in Holland. Her own behavior was childlike, for she seemed incapable of thinking of anything beyond her own immediate desires. The principles that had led the Separatists to seek a new life on a strange continent, thousands of miles from the world they knew, meant nothing to her. She was only a few years older than Priscilla, who carried herself with the dignity and grace of a woman. Dorothy, Susanna reflected, was someone who might never really mature.

Sobs racked Dorothy's slender frame, and as she became conscious of the commotion she was making, she bent her head over her laundry, bit her lower lip and tried to control her weeping.

Susanna put a hand on her friend's arm. "Dorothy," she said, "all of us are frightened, you know. I'm sure that no one can say what lies ahead for us — not Elder Brewster or Governor Carver or even your husband. But, no matter what may be in store, we've got to make the best of things. We made our choice when we sailed on the *Mayflower*."

"That's right," Priscilla declared. "It does no good to look back now. We must forget yesterday and live for today — and tomorrow."

Dorothy heard neither of them as she pounded some of Bradford's clothes with a rock in a futile attempt to rid herself of a helpless, unreasoning sense of rage.

The days passed slowly. Everyone was heartily sick of life aboard the *Mayflower*, but the colonists were destined to spend the better part of a month on the ship before they would finally begin moving ashore. The search for a permanent site on which to build a town seemed endless, and at times even the strongest, most optimistic men — like Bradford and Winslow and Standish — suffered pangs of doubt and the longboat, or shallop, that the Pilgrims had brought with them so they could fish and make short voyages of exploration was carried onto the beach and repaired. In the days that followed, the men went ashore in groups of sixteen at a time, the capacity of the boat. They marched across the countryside, systematically exploring all of Cape Cod. The more impatient were so anxious to settle on dry land that they repeatedly urged their comrades to accept spots that were obviously inferior.

But Bradford held firm. "Wait," he told them. "Someday — soon, I hope — we'll find the place we want."

One morning the men came across some strange, man-made hillocks, the first signs that the Cape was inhabited. They dug into the hillocks, and there found a number of baskets filled with corn seed. They were so jubilant that they carried ten bushels of the seed to the *Mayflower*, rejoicing because they would be able to plant a bountiful crop when they decided on a place to settle.

But Elder Brewster looked at them in horror. "You've stolen seed that belongs to the natives," he told them sternly. Bradford knew he was right, and flushed.

Some of the others were more brazen. "We need all the food we can find if we hope to survive," one said.

"The Indians should take better care of property if they don't want to lose it," another declared.

The Elder shook his head sorrowfully and walked away down the deck.

Bradford held up a hand for silence. "The day will soon come when we meet the natives," he told the colonists. "I propose that we tell them at once we've taken the corn — and offer them anything they want in return."

"Not firearms," Standish said hastily. "Under no circumstances must we allow savages to gain possession of blunderbusses and ammunition and gunpowder! Our own safety depends on the superiority of our weapons."

The others nodded in agreement.

"Very well," Bradford said with a frown. "But if we hope to live as friendly neighbors, we must be honest. Captain John Smith says in his book that they place a high value on blankets and knives. So, when we meet the Indians, we must offer them a fair trade."

The men who were members of the Separatist church agreed, but Standish felt dubious. Savages, he thought, were not rational, and he believed it far more likely they would attack the intruders than sit down to bargain with strangers from across the sea.

Cape Cod is shaped like a large half-circle, and when no site appropriate for the establishment of a permanent settlement was found near the *Mayflower*'s anchorage, the men decided to explore the opposite side of the bay. There, according to the detailed and accurate map John Smith had made in 1614, was a river running into a good harbor. Smith had named the spot New Plymouth.

A party of sixteen set out in the shallop early in the morning of December 6. Everyone had realized that time was important if a place was to be located and houses built, for winter was approaching. The weather that day emphasized the urgency of the mission. A bitter cold numbed them, a sharp wind cut through their clothes, and icy spray drenched them.

But Captain Standish, who was in command of the party, did not think of returning to the relative warmth of the *Mayflower*. The shallop held to its course, using Smith's chart, and at last approached the rocky beach.

Bradford, seated in the prow, called out softly and pointed. The men could scarcely contain their excitement when they saw a party of Indians, dressed in deerskins, gathered around a large black object on the beach. When the boat headed for the shore the savages ran off. The Pilgrims, beaching the shallop, discovered that the natives had been cutting up an enormous fish, about fifteen feet long, with flesh somewhat similar to that of a swine.

The forest behind the beach was thick. A roaring fire was built on the sand, and at Standish's direction a crude barricade of stakes, driftwood logs and boughs was erected. The Indians did not reappear, and the party cautiously explored the land behind the beach. There they found good soil and a swiftly flowing stream of clear water in which they saw trout. Standish and Bradford agreed that a hill behind the rock-strewn beach, overlooking the harbor, was a natural site for a fort. The woods were rich in elm and oak, maple and pine.

It was too late to return to the *Mayflower*, so the fire was built higher, and the men roasted some of the edible portions of the huge fish. Sentries took up posts at the barricades, and Standish made certain that every blunderbuss was loaded before anyone went to sleep beside the fire.

In the middle of the night the company was awakened by loud, shrill cries from the forest. The sentries immediately fired their blunderbusses into the darkness. One of the *Mayflower*'s sailors, who was serving as a member of the shallop's crew, told the others that the alarming sound was merely the howling of wolves, so everyone settled down again for the rest of the night.

Bradford believed the right site had been found at last, and John Carver, who had been elected governor of the colony, agreed with him. They decided to return to the *Mayflower* with the good news as quickly as possible. So, while several members of the expedition roasted generous slices of the fish for breakfast, others began to carry their supplies down to the shallop.

Captain Standish, who was throwing pieces of driftwood onto the fire, stopped and shouted at three of the men. "What are you doing with your flintlocks?"

"Taking them down to the boat so we can wrap them before we sail," one replied.

The Captain frowned. "Under no circumstances should you be separated from your firearms!"

The trio ignored him and walked off down the beach.

Standish wanted to make an issue of the affair, but was dissuaded by Carver, who hated disputes. He agreed in principle with the Captain's position, he said, but added that the extreme cold required everyone to be practical. "We can discuss the question of discipline later," he said. "Right now I suggest we eat and go. We'll all be in the shallop in another few minutes."

The three who had disobeyed Standish returned from the boat without their weapons, and the company sat down to eat a hasty breakfast. But the meal was interrupted when a shower of arrows fell on the men huddled around the fire. The early morning silence was broken by loud, taunting cries.

Standish snatched his blunderbuss and fired it in the direction of the forest. John Howland immediately did the same. The Indians continued to shout from behind the cover of trees as Winslow, Carver and several others also fired. But the shots were ineffective, and the arrows continued to fall.

Bradford's gun jammed, much to his disgust, and he struggled with it feverishly until he heard Carver call out in dismay. Looking up, he saw the three disobedient colonists running toward the shallop to retrieve their firearms. Standish and Carver called to them to return. But the renegades, hoping to make up for their error, increased their speed.

Several savages clad in skins, their faces smeared with paint, broke out of the forest and started after the trio. For an instant Bradford was paralyzed by fear, yet he knew what he had to do. He felt only contempt for the three men whose recklessness jeopardized the whole group, but his dedicated sense of duty gave him no choice.

Throwing aside his worthless flintlock, Bradford drew his sword and dashed toward the savages. Two or three others quickly followed him. The Indians turned, ready for close combat, but the sight of his long, double-edged blade frightened them, and they raced back toward the forest.

A volley of shots hastened their flight. Standish, firing with cool precision, sent a ball crashing into the trunk of a sapling only a few inches from the face of the leader of the attacking band. The savage shrieked and retreated, and his men scattered, crashing through the underbrush in their panic.

The brief battle was over, and the members of the expedition gathered around the fire. Bradford caught his breath as he looked at the others. "This is not the time for speeches," he said firmly. "But it must be plain now to all of you that if we hope to survive, every one of us must exercise self-discipline. For the sake of our families, our whole future, we must do what we're told."

7

The members of the expedition climbed up the ladder onto the deck of the *Mayflower*, shouting the good news to the weary men and women who were waiting for them. They had found the right site for their settlement and had driven off a party of hostile savages. Each of the men was surrounded as he came onto the deck, and everyone talked at once.

Elder Brewster stood apart from the others, his face grave. He made no move until he saw Bradford climb onto the deck, then he stepped forward, beckoning. The hubbub subsided, then resumed as Brewster led his friend forward to a deserted portion of the deck.

Bradford, eager to describe New Plymouth, started to speak, but Brewster silenced him. "We'll discuss these matters later."

Something in his tone caused Bradford to pause. "What's wrong?"

"Brace yourself for dreadful news." The older man pointed toward the prow. "She was last seen standing there."

Bradford stared at him blankly.

"Dorothy disappeared into the waters of the bay."

The shock was so intense that Bradford looked as though he would faint.

"Captain Jones and his men have spent hours searching for her. Perhaps she carried heavy weights in her clothing, for she hasn't risen to the surface." Brewster kept a tight grip on his friend's arm.

"Are you suggesting — that it wasn't an accident?" Bradford scarcely recognized his own hoarse, strained voice.

"I don't know. No one does. I took the liberty of examining her belongings, but she left no note, no message. Perhaps she fell overboard, perhaps she jumped." Brewster spoke sorrowfully. "It's useless to speculate, William. The Lord gives, the Lord takes away."

The sky overhead was dark, gloomy, but Bradford felt the glare reflected by the water and covered his eyes with his hands. As his first sense of shock and disbelief subsided, a feeling of horror crept over him. He felt positive that the unhappy, bewildered Dorothy had taken her own life. No matter what the Elder said, she could not have fallen overboard accidentally. She had been too miserable for too long.

Unexpectedly, suddenly, a sob welled up in Bradford.

"The Lord gives, and the Lord takes away," Elder Brewster repeated.

She had been too young to die, Bradford told himself. And he had been at fault for insisting that she accompany him to these bleak New World shores. She would be alive at this moment if he had allowed her to remain in Holland.

It was true that he had not loved her, any more than she had loved him. Only one woman had ever received his love, but he could not think of Alice now — or ever again. Dorothy had been his wife, the mother of his son. And now she was gone.

Tears rolled down his cheeks, but he made no attempt to wipe them away, and continued to stand with his hands over his face.

The Elder gave him a few moments to compose himself. "I know you must mourn, William, but you can't allow yourself to look back."

"Are you asking me to forget her?" Bradford demanded bitterly.

"No, I'm not foolish enough to suggest that you will ever forget this tragedy," Brewster said. "You'll remember it all of your days, and your grief will always be a part of you. But you must think of tomorrow, not today. You must help yourself, William, and the rest of us need you, too. I beg you to discipline yourself."

Only a few hours earlier, on the beach at New Plymouth, Bradford had demanded that everyone exercise self-discipline. Now, ironically, he would be the first to have to practice what he had preached. He shuddered, let his hand fall to his side and, very slowly, very painfully, forced himself to stand erect.

The *Mayflower* sailed across the bay, and the colonists went to work with a vengeance soon after the anchor was dropped. Trees were felled and fashioned into planks. Then squads working under John Alden's direction built the skeleton framework for the first building to be erected, the Common House. The walls were filled in with "wattle and daub," reeds mixed with clay, and a thatched roof was hammered into place.

Ground was cleared at the top of the hill for a fort, and men worked ceaselessly, in spite of the bitter cold. Hunting parties went off into the forests to search for game, and other groups went fishing in the shallop. Neither enjoyed good fortune. Snow fell frequently, and the cold was more intense than any the Pilgrims had ever known. But the work did not slacken, and everyone contributed a fair share. Of necessity, the whole company continued to live on board the *Mayflower*. It would not be possible until spring to move to the houses that were slowly taking shape.

But spring seemed far away. People continued to subsist, in the main, on provisions they had carried with them from England and Holland. Occasionally the fishermen brought in a cod or a tuna, and twice speared one of the enormous black fish, which the settlers called "the howling whale." Now and again Standish and his hunters enjoyed good luck, too, and came back from the forests with a deer. It was impossible to feed so many on these delicacies, however, and the diet remained bleak.

Ground could not be broken for planting until the weather became warmer, and at the moment it was impossible to do more than chop down the beech and ash trees on the plots where planting would be done. Even that effort was discouraging, for the earth remained frozen.

A mysterious ailment which not even Sam Fuller could diagnose almost wiped out the fledgling colony. The symptoms were always the same. People ran a fever, lost their appetites and soon became too weak to stand. For want of a better name, the disease was called, simply, "the sickness." It took a terrible toll, killing children and women as well as men, and virtually every family suffered losses. Susanna White, Sam Fuller's sister, lost her husband, William. Priscilla Mullins was orphaned when both of her parents and her brother were carried away.

Those who recovered discovered they were spiritually stronger than before. They had been tested in a fiercely burning crucible, and when they regained their health they were determined to remain in the New World. Not one wanted to go back to England or Holland on the *Mayflower*.

The best that could be said of the terrible winter of 1620-21 was that the Indians of Cape Cod kept their distance from New Plymouth. Standish and his hunters encountered small parties of warriors in the forests now and again, but the savages swiftly disappeared. It was apparent that they were afraid of the settlers' firearms and had no intention of attacking men who carried such potent weapons. Nevertheless the colonists took no unnecessary chances. They always kept their flintlocks nearby when working on shore, and at night, no matter how cold the weather, sentries stood guard duty.

Then, one afternoon in late February something happened that, everyone agreed, was even more remarkable than the rescue of John Howland from the sea.

William Bradford and Edward Winslow had been cutting wood for the first of the private houses, which was being constructed for Elder Brewster and his family. Thoroughly chilled after spending hours at hard labor in the open, they went down to the rocky beach and lighted a fire. They stood before it, warming themselves, when suddenly Winslow saw someone coming down the beach toward them.

For a few moments they thought the man was one of their own company, and not until he had drawn near did they realize he was an Indian. They gaped at him in wonder, reaching for their flintlocks belatedly; never had they seen anyone in such a strange jumble of clothing.

The Indian, who appeared to be in his late thirties, was a short, heavy-set man with high cheekbones, copper-colored skin and exceptionally large, black eyes. He was wearing fringed buckskin trousers, moccasins of soft leather, and a large native amulet was suspended from a thong around his neck. But on his head was a battered, plumed hat of European make, a short gentleman's cloak fell from his shoulders, and the upper part of his body was encased in a frayed velvet cloak with tarnished metal buttons.

The warrior removed his hat in a sweeping gesture and bowed low. "Squanto gives greetings to new friends," he said. "Welcome to New England."

Bradford and Winslow glanced at each other, uncertain whether they were dreaming or going mad. The brave had addressed them in English, and his accent was unmistakably that of London's lower class. Even more bewildering, he had used the name, New England, which Captain John Smith had given the area.

"Squanto pleased to find brothers in this land." The brave smiled broadly and extended his right hand, as civilized men did. "Tribes say Squanto Englishman now. Squanto think so, too. So come to live with new friends."

Gradually Bradford and Winslow recovered from their astonishment and completely forgot the biting cold as Squanto told them his incredible story. Fifteen years earlier, in 1605, he had gone off to England with Captain George Weymouth, an explorer who had visited Cape Cod. He had spent nine years in England, then had returned home with Captain Smith in 1614. Soon thereafter he had been kidnapped, along with several other natives, by one of Smith's lieutenants, Thomas Hunt. The unscrupulous Hunt had taken the Indians to Spain and had sold them there as slaves. Squanto's knowledge of English had brought him to the attention of a friendly priest, who had procured his freedom.

After many adventures he had returned to England and had stayed there until 1619, when another explorer, Captain Thomas Dermer, had brought him back to Cape Cod, his home. On his arrival he had found that his entire tribe, the Pawtuxet, had died of a plague. Alone and friendless, he had wandered through the area for months. Recently other Indians had told him of the settlers' arrival, so he had come to make his home with them.

The Pilgrims instantly recognized Squanto's value to the colony. Now they had an interpreter and go-between who could help them establish friendly relations with the tribes who had been hostile to them.

The entire company extended a hearty welcome to Squanto. He, in turn, was delighted to resume a way of life he had learned in England, for he had outgrown the primitive customs of his own people.

Bradford summed up the feelings of everyone when he said, "Squanto is a special instrument sent to us by the Almighty for our mutual good, and beyond our expectation."

Squanto soon proved his worth. When the weather became warmer, he showed the settlers how to set traps for the herring that ran in great numbers up the river. Then he taught them to plant their corn in small hillocks, eighteen inches apart, using herring as fertilizer. He advised them to station guards in the fields to keep away the wolves. He took the hunters to salt licks where deer were often found. And he showed the women how to make pliable fish nets of birch roots.

The children were fascinated by Squanto, and he returned their friendship, taking them to secret places in the forest where they could fill countless baskets with plump raspberries and strawberries. Housewives were happy when he brought their sons and daughters home carrying watercress found on the banks of small streams, large stores of onions and leeks, and a variety of herbs that made cooking less of a chore and eating more of a pleasure.

Gradually the settlement, now called Plymouth, began to take form. Captain Standish built a platform on the top of the hill for his cannon, and work was started on the Fort. Houses lined both sides of the town's first thoroughfare, the Street, which extended from the hill to the beach. The men and older boys worked feverishly, and before long a second street, which bisected the first, was laid out. It was called the Road.

Planting of corn was begun under Squanto's supervision, and seeds brought from Holland were placed in the earth, too. Soon, the Pilgrims told each other, they would be eating cabbages and turnips and peas, parsnips and beans. And Squanto introduced them to a gourd-like Indian plant, which grew along the ground on vines. He called it *asquutasquash*, and the children, unable to pronounce such a long word, soon shortened its name to squash.

One day in April, while some of the men were laboring in the fields under the warmest sun they had yet felt in the New World, fate again intervened. Governor John Carver, one of the kindest and most gentle of men, died suddenly of a heart attack while digging up a tree stump. No one yet knew it, but his passing was destined to change the entire atmosphere of Plymouth.

That evening, at sundown, the leaderless men gathered at the Common House. No one had summoned them, but instinct had prompted their meeting. Everyone was worried, and the light shed by four candles seemed to emphasize the lines at the corners of their mouths, the smudges beneath their eyes. They crowded into the single, bare room of the Common House, and someone suggested that Elder Brewster act as chairman.

"I must decline," he told them. "As I'm your spiritual leader until Pastor Robinson joins us, I can take no part in the civil administration of this colony."

Those who had suffered because of their belief that church and state should remain separate agreed with him emphatically.

"Our course of action seems obvious to me, as it does to several of you with whom I've talked," Edward Winslow said. "I propose that we elect Master William Bradford as governor."

John Alden raised his voice. "I suggest we make his election unanimous!"

The entire company cheered, and the startled Bradford was pushed to the front of the room. He felt humble, and a sense of panic assailed him. Others, he thought, were more worthy. Winslow was a better diplomat, Fuller was more tolerant, Alden possessed greater skill.

On the other hand, his one concern since Dorothy's death had been the future of Plymouth. It would be wrong to stand aside when he was being offered the opportunity to make the settlement prosperous and secure.

"I accept the office," he said, and even the nonchurch members, who sometimes grumbled that Separatists loved long conversations, had to admit they had never heard a shorter speech.

The people of Plymouth soon discovered that life was vastly different under the stern guidance of a young and energetic governor. Daily work schedules were drawn up for the men, others were made for the women, and even the children were assigned specific duties. Everyone labored from dawn until dusk, except on the Sabbath. Bradford, whose energy seemed inexhaustible, set an example, often working far into the night.

By late spring the Fort was taking shape, and nineteen Sturdy houses had been completed. The corn and other crops were tended with great care, and Bradford, along with others who had been farmers, spent twelve hours and longer in the fields each day. Deer and rabbits were caught in Squanto's many snares, and thanks to his instruction, the luck of the fishermen improved.

It appeared that the colony could stand on its own feet at last. The *Mayflower*'s seamen were anxious to return to England,

and although Captain Jones was reluctant to leave the people who had become his close friends, he agreed to sail.

The holds were filled with prime lumber which would earn a substantial profit for the colony's financial supporters in London. Casks of fresh water were taken on board, and the settlers presented Jones with three large, freshly caught cod as a parting gift.

Bradford gave anyone who wanted to return to England or Holland the right to go. But, in spite of all the hardships the settlers had endured, in spite of their knowledge that the road ahead was difficult, the people unanimously agreed to stay.

Everyone came down to the rocky beach for a last farewell. There was no ceremony, and no speeches were made. A sailor collected letters for relatives on the far side of the Atlantic, and Captain Jones shook the hands of his friends. Then he had himself rowed out to his ship. The anchor was hoisted, sails were raised and, as the *Mayflower* glided out of Plymouth harbor, Standish's cannon boomed a final salute.

The little company on shore watched until the ship that had been their refuge and home vanished over the horizon. Then they were alone in the vast wilderness of the unknown New World.

8

Edward Winslow was anxious to learn the language of the Indians, and took lessons from Squanto. He soon acquired considerable skill, but had no opportunity to practice his new talents, for the natives of Cape Cod continued to avoid the settlers. In the meantime, the colonists did not relax their vigilance. A palisade was built to protect the fields and homes of the settlers, and men mounted guard duty day and night.

Governor Bradford believed it was essential to come to terms with the local tribes. He urged Squanto to travel to the towns of the Wampanoag, the most powerful and prosperous of the Indian nations, and tell the natives that the newcomers wanted to be their friends. But Squanto refused.

"When Wampanoag ready," he said, "maybe Chief Massasoyt come to Plymouth. Maybe send brave. Until Wampanoag ready, nobody come."

Not until early in the summer of 1621 did a warrior appear at Plymouth's new gates. He was a tall, solidly built man, dressed only in a loincloth, carrying a bone-handled knife in his belt, with a strong bow and a quiver filled with arrows slung over one shoulder. Winslow hurried to meet him, and Squanto, who went to the gate, too, was indignant.

"Hobomok, *pinese* of Wampanoag, come to live in Plymouth!" he said to Governor Bradford, angry because he was afraid his own special position would be undermined.

Bradford and Winslow were elated, however. Hobomok, a *pinese*, or lord, of the Wampanoag nation, had been sent as an ambassador to the colony. The ice had been broken, and aside from Squanto, only Miles Standish was unhappy. "He's come here to spy on us," the Captain said.

Bradford had already considered that possibility. "Squanto is so jealous he'll keep a sharp watch on the warrior."

"That won't be enough," Standish replied. "Squanto is living at your house. He can't keep a constant eye on the man."

Bradford smiled. "Suppose Hobomok stays with you, Miles? Then you can watch him yourself."

The Captain groaned. "Let him stay with Edward Winslow, the only colonist who understands the talk of Indians well enough to know what Hobomok says."

Bradford suppressed a chuckle.

Standish glowered. "All right, I'll speak the truth. I don't look forward to sharing a little cottage with someone who coats his hair with rancid fish oil and his body with stale meat fat!" All at once his belligerence vanished. "I'll do it," he said. "I realize that Squanto and Hobomok must be kept apart so they don't cut each other's throats before they learn to live side by side in the same community."

"That won't happen," Bradford assured him. "Hobomok looks down on Squanto. And Squanto is more eager than ever to keep our favor, so he won't do anything rash. The one real danger is that Hobomok's master has sent him here to learn about us so the Indians will be better able to attack us."

"Never fear," Standish growled. "I won't let him near our weapons. As for our daily habits, I don't see how we can conceal anything from him."

"We can't," Bradford said soberly. "We're taking a risk, but I'm afraid we have no choice. We can't live permanently under siege conditions. We must either persuade the Wampanoag to become our friends, or the day will come when they and their allies will join forces and drive us into the sea."

The problems of obtaining enough food and of establishing friendly relations with the Indians were the principal concerns of the settlers through the long, hot summer of 1621.

Bradford had good reason to hope there would be more than enough to eat. Rain had been plentiful, crops were ripening and the forests continued to yield large quantities of berries, onions and edible roots, which Squanto and Hobomok taught the colonists to find. The skill of the hunters improved, and the fishermen, learning from practice, had discovered their catch increased greatly when they fashioned small hooks for sea bass and used reinforced nets when they went out for cod.

The realization dawned gradually that, after spending nine months in the New World, English townsmen were becoming acclimated to the wilderness. The forest was no longer frightening, but a source of food and shelter. The sea, when treated with respect, was generous. People who had survived "the sickness" and the bleak cold of an unusually frigid Cape Cod winter had become stronger, more resilient.

The men were no longer tired after spending all day in the fields, in the shallop or tramping through deep woods. The women cooked and sewed and cleaned, took care of their children and tended their kitchen gardens of vegetables and herbs. The youngsters spent the better part of each day in the school Bradford had established for them. But they had regularly scheduled work assignments, too. The boys scoured the shallow waters off the beach for crabs, mussels and clams. The girls picked berries. The smaller children became adept at mending fishing nets. And everyone under the age of seventeen soon became an expert swimmer.

At dusk every evening the men reported to Standish for militia duty, and no one was exempt. The Captain taught them how to care for their weapons, march and maneuver. Twice each week there was target practice with muskets and pistols. The cannon in the Fort were not fired, however, for they required too much gunpowder, which was carefully hoarded.

Hobomok made three journeys to the main town of the Wampanoag, accompanied by a vigilant Squanto and by Winslow, who carried gifts of knives, mirrors and blankets to the savages. Massasoyt, the chief of the tribe, promised to visit Plymouth soon, and the colony's leaders felt reasonably sure that their neighbors would sign a treaty of peace.

Then, in September, the settlers suddenly found themselves trapped between opposing forces when a fierce Indian war erupted. The Massachusetts, a great and powerful nation whose domain was north of Cape Cod, went on the warpath against the Wampanoag, their traditional enemies. They were joined by the Nemasket, the most ferocious of the Cape tribes. Its chief, Corbitant, was ambitious. Three warriors of a small, neutral tribe stopped off at Plymouth one day to report they had heard a startling rumor. It was being said that Corbitant had captured Chief Massasoyt.

If the story was true, there would be chaos everywhere, as Massasoyt was the only man strong enough to prevent the many lesser nations from squabbling. Plymouth could not hope to escape if a general war broke out. Most of the savages would be eager to destroy the foreigners.

Bradford sent Hobomok and Squanto into the interior to investigate the rumor. Two days later Hobomok returned. Massasoyt had not been kidnapped, he said. But the Nemasket had captured Squanto, had held him for a few hours, and before he had managed to escape, Corbitant had been heard to boast that Plymouth was his real foe. By killing his two captives, he would deprive the settlers of their eyes and voice.

Then he would attack the town, kill the men and make the women and children his slaves. Hobomok had no idea whether Squanto was dead or alive.

Plymouth moved swiftly to meet the crisis. Standish, accompanied by seventeen settlers, all heavily armed, started out at once on a march to the main village of the Nemasket. Hobomok led the party. The men demonstrated, in this hour of emergency, that they had indeed adapted to the wilderness. They searched the forest carefully for potential enemies as they advanced, and they avoided dead branches that littered the ground and other underbrush that might crackle beneath their feet. They made frequent detours around bramble patches and fallen trees without reducing their speed.

At dusk, after marching more than eight hours, they halted for a brief rest. The advance was resumed as night fell, and Hobomok maintained the same steady pace until they reached a knoll only a short distance from the Nemasket village. Then he halted, and the colonists studied the sleeping community by the light of a rising three-quarter moon.

The hut of Corbitant, a flimsy structure of dried reeds and animal skins, was the largest building in the town. Standish decided to concentrate his attack on it. No one knew how many braves might be in the village, so his plan was simple and direct. If the chief could be captured, he could be held as a hostage. Then his warriors would refrain from counterattacking for fear the Englishmen would kill their leader.

There were two entrances to the hut, so Standish divided his company. Four men were placed under Bradford's command, with orders to bar the small opening at the rear. The larger group would storm the main entrance and demand that Corbitant surrender or suffer the consequences. Bradford and his companions obeyed at once, and silently crept down into the village.

The houses stood in a circle inside a clearing, and the Nemasket did not stir as the five colonists drew closer to the chief's house. But there was a strong possibility that someone would awaken, see the colonists and raise an alarm before either of the two parties reached Corbitant's house on the far rim of the circle.

Suddenly a dog barked.

The five men froze, and after a moment or two the dog fell silent. But, as soon as the squad started forward again, the animal resumed its furious challenge. Bradford knew he had to keep going. His only hope of avoiding discovery lay in the possibility that the Nemasket, who had many dogs, would ignore the noise. The band remained behind a cover of trees and finally reached the hut. There the men crouched low so their silhouettes would not reveal their presence in the moonlight.

Time dragged interminably as the settlers waited for the larger party to reach the front of the hut. Standish and his men had a longer, more difficult assignment. Hobomok had to lead them through the center of the village, past stone-lined cooking pits and platforms built for funeral services.

Moving with the cautious grace of a wild beast stalking its prey, Hobomok seemed to glide across the open compound. Standish, who was directly behind him, made more noise than any other member of the party. The pounding of his boots on the hard-packed, dry ground sounded like thunder to the tense men hiding behind the hut.

At last the larger squad approached the front entrance. The men were formed into a semicircle, their muskets cocked, and

Standish stepped forward with Hobomok. "Corbitant!" the Captain shouted. "Come out!"

Hobomok translated the demand and added an insult of his own.

There was a stir inside the hut, then the attackers heard a babble of excited voices. But no one came out. Displaying more courage than common sense, Standish pushed aside the entrance flap and stalked inside. "I want Corbitant," he roared, "to punish him for the murder of our friend, Squanto!"

The frightened, confused savages could not understand a word he said, and there was a sudden rush for the rear. Three warriors emerged into the open, and Bradford cried, "Fire!"

Five muskets spoke at almost the same instant, and two of the warriors fell, one with a wound in the leg, the other with a bullet in the thigh. The third ducked back into the hut, and Hobomok shouted triumphantly as he grasped Corbitant's scalp lock.

Corbitant, a wiry man with long arms, wriggled in his captor's grasp as he spoke rapidly.

Winslow understood enough of the native language to translate. "He says Squanto is alive!"

"Have him brought here immediately," Standish commanded.

A Nemasket boy in his early teens sprinted away. The whole village was stirring now, and warriors and squaws who emerged from other buildings were huddling together, muttering when they saw that their chief was a prisoner. Apparently the braves had no intention of fighting, but Standish was not taking any chances, and the colonists were ready to fire a volley at the first sign of a rush.

Soon Squanto appeared, calm and smiling. His friends were astonished to see him alive and well, but he explained he had persuaded his captors to spare his life. Long experience with desperate situations had given him a glib tongue, and he appeared to be indestructible.

The crisis ended as abruptly as it had arisen. While Sam Fuller removed the bullets from the bodies of the two injured warriors and treated their wounds, Corbitant swore he would be the friend of Plymouth as long as he lived. He promised, too, to make peace with the Wampanoag.

Bradford and Standish were skeptical, afraid that he would break his pledge as soon as they left, but Squanto was certain the chief meant what he said. "Corbitant keep word," he declared. "Corbitant afraid of English magic."

Squanto lowered his voice. "Nemasket stupid people. Corbitant most stupid. All believe big lie. Squanto tell that English bury plague under Common House. First Squanto say English brothers send plague to Nemasket if Squanto die. Squanto live. Now Squanto say English send plague if Nemasket make war. So Nemasket make peace. Corbitant very afraid, so keep promise for all time."

Bradford had to curb a desire to smile. Precious ammunition and gunpowder were kept in watertight boxes in a cellar the colonists had dug beneath their Common House.

But the results of the raid were far too important to be amusing. Squanto's lively imagination and intimate knowledge of Indian superstitions, combined with the colonists' courage and swift reaction to a threat, had smashed Corbitant's alliance with the Massachusetts. Above all, the Wampanoag now had concrete proof that the settlers wanted to be their friends, and certainly would respond in kind.

The raid on the village of the Nemasket produced consequences more far-reaching than anyone in Plymouth expected. Within a week of the military expedition's return, representatives of all nine Cape Cod tribes came to Plymouth bearing gifts of venison, quail and flounder, a fish the colonists had not yet eaten. The natives sued for peace, swearing they wanted to become the brothers of the settlers.

Their offers were accepted, and they were given gifts in return. Then arrangements were made with them to trade blankets, knives and other articles for furs and food. Bradford, ever conscious of the power of the Wampanoag, insisted that his visitors obey Massasoyt as their overlord. The spokesmen for the other tribes accepted his demand without hesitation.

The gesture pleased Hobomok, who went off to tell Massasoyt the good news. With him he carried an invitation to visit Plymouth, and he returned in a few days with an acceptance. His chief and the senior warriors of the Wampanoag would come to Plymouth, he said, when the autumn harvest had been gathered.

Word of the potency of English firearms, which were far stronger "magic" than Squanto's imaginary plague-in-a-box, reached the Massachusetts, and they sued for peace, too. The victory achieved by the raid on the Nemasket was now complete.

The establishment of relationships with the Massachusetts produced immediate commercial results. This wealthy nation used the pelts of beaver and fox as media of exchange, and Bradford traveled north in the shallop to visit them. He struck bargains that satisfied both sides, and returned to Plymouth with the boat filled almost to overflowing with bales of prime beaver. When another ship came to Plymouth, it would return to England laden with enough furs to make a substantial reduction in the Separatists' debt to their financial supporters.

Autumn came, Plymouth reaped its first harvest, and the twenty acres of native corn that had been planted yielded an abundant quantity of grain. The sea teemed with fish; the deer hunts were successful. The grapes had ripened, and there was an abundance of onions, watercress and leeks.

For the first time since the settlers had landed, almost a year ago, there was more than enough to eat. The crops of Dutch peas, barley and wheat were poor, but for the moment no one cared. The people wanted some tangible way to express their joy, and thought it would be appropriate to hold a ceremony in which everyone would share.

Elder Brewster remembered a custom that the Dutch observed, which they in turn had learned from the Jews, to whom they had granted freedom of religion. He searched through his Bible, and in the Book of Psalms, in Isaiah and in Amos he found references to the ancient practice of offering thanks to God for providing His children with enough food to sustain them.

So a proclamation was issued, stating that a harvest festival would be held in two weeks. It would be preceded by a special religious service, to which Separatist church members and non-members alike were invited. It had become a custom for those who did not belong to the church to remain at home while religious services were conducted on the Sabbath, for the Separatists allowed no public services other than their own.

Men and women who had been persecuted and driven from England because of their religious beliefs were making certain that their faith took root in the New World soil. Non-Separatists could worship as they pleased in the privacy of their homes. But the special service would be something different.

It would appeal to all, Elder Brewster told the people. He emphasized, too, that differences in faith were not important.

Everyone believed in the same God, and all were urged to offer their gratitude for His bounty.

Governor Bradford decided the occasion was appropriate for the long-awaited meeting with Massasoyt, and Hobomok was sent to the main Wampanoag town to extend the settlers' hospitality to his chief.

Two days later Massasoyt appeared at Plymouth. A tall, stately man with a proud bearing, he looked and behaved like the great prince he was. He and Bradford liked each other at once, and the Governor was the host at a small party for the chief of the Wampanoag and the three braves who had accompanied him.

A few days before the festival, the women of Plymouth began to prepare feverishly for the event. Cooking fires were lighted early in the morning and burned until long after dark. Then, two days before the banquet, Susanna Winslow and Priscilla Mullins, who was now Mrs. Alden, came to Bradford with tears in their eyes, so upset that at first neither could speak.

"Squanto has just told us," Susanna said, almost choking on her words, "that ninety Wampanoag warriors are marching here through the forest. He says they're Massasoyt's guard of honor, and they expect to join us at the feast."

Priscilla was even more disturbed. "We don't have enough food for that many people. What on earth shall we do?"

Bradford solved the problem by explaining the situation frankly to his guest. So Massasoyt sent his men hunting. They came back with three fat bucks and two does, a flock of geese and fifteen swordfish. They also knew where to find wild plums and tiny, sweet apples, and soon larders were overflowing.

In all, the Indians contributed several times as much food as they themselves could consume. That night the women worked past midnight.

The ceremonies began on the morning of the festival with a worship service. The Indians attended out of curiosity, and Squanto translated Elder Brewster's brief, simple sermon. Everyone than trooped out into the open. Standish, who never missed an opportunity to impress savages with the power of his firearms, held a military review that ended with a deafening volley of cannon fire.

The colonists and their guests retired to the beach, where the young men of Plymouth and the Wampanoag warriors tested their strength and speed. They held wrestling matches, races and knife-throwing contests, and both winners and losers were applauded.

The air was bracing, and in mid-afternoon the ravenous company returned to the Fort, the only building in the town large enough to accommodate such a throng. There the last-minute preparations were speeded; then the unmarried men and some of the younger braves helped the women and girls carry huge platters of food into the main chamber. The settlers and the Indians, seated at long, rough-hewn tables, cheered loudly.

The whole company fell silent as Elder Brewster thanked the Almighty for His generosity. Then the colonist who sat at the head of each table carved the many different kinds of meat set before him. The warriors were dumbfounded by this strange custom — they tore meat apart with their hands — but they watched and learned. Soon they, like the people of Plymouth, were spearing chunks of food on their knives.

Family groups chatted vivaciously, and no one was happier than those who had made new lives for themselves. Most of the widows and widowers had remarried, and the occasion was significant for them; they remembered the tragedies they had suffered, but they looked toward the future with confidence.

At the end of the meal, the dishes were cleared away, and the settlers drank a toast to their new friends, the Wampanoag. There were still a few surprises in store. Hobomok, grinning broadly, gave the children lumps of candy made with sugar that had been extracted from the roots of wild beet plants. Then the adults exchanged gifts. Bradford presented Massasoyt with a bolt of cloth and received a beaver cloak in return. The warriors received iron cooking pots and strings of brightly colored beads. They responded by going out beyond the palisade, then returning with several deer they had killed the previous day. The meat would be smoked in order to preserve it and would be added to the store that would see the settlers through the coming winter.

When the ceremonies were completed, Elder Brewster stood to deliver the benediction. *"I thank my God upon every remembrance of you,"* he said, quoting from the Bible. *"Every creature of God is good, and nothing is to be refused, if it be received with thanksgiving."*

From that time forward, a similar celebration was held each year, in the autumn, and was known as the festival of Thanksgiving.

9

Late in November, 1621, a heavy snowfall blanketed Plymouth. The colonists, grateful for their snug houses, supplies of firewood and provisions, prepared to settle down for the winter. A few days later it began to snow again, and Hobomok and Squanto went into the forest before the drifts became too deep, to inspect some snares they had set.

They returned hurriedly, however, to say they had caught a glimpse of a ship sailing toward the harbor. An alarm was sounded, and the militia made ready to repel hostile invaders. But the atmosphere changed to one of wonder and joy when Hobomok, who was staring out of a window of the Fort with Captain Standish, announced, "White flag with red cross." The ship was English, and soon they could read her name, the *Fortune.*

Everyone hurried down to the beach. After spending a full year in the New World, the settlers hoped to receive mail from home. There might well be friends and relatives on board, and certainly there would be supplies of all sorts in the hold.

The first ashore was Robert Cushman, a Separatist leader who had been forced to remain behind the previous year when the *Speedwell* had been abandoned. He was followed by thirty-five others, many of them relatives of the original colonists and most of them Separatist friends.

The reunion was a happy occasion. Everyone listened intently as Elder Brewster read aloud a letter from Pastor Robinson. The clergyman offered his condolences for the settlers' losses, and expressed the hope that he and the members of the congregation still in Holland could come to Plymouth soon.

Cushman went off with Bradford to the Governor's house for a private conference, saying that he intended to return to Europe on the *Fortune*, to help others prepare for the migration.

Bradford glanced through the window at the *Fortune*, riding at anchor in the harbor. "Neither you nor the master of the ship has shown me a list of her cargo as yet," he said, prodding gently.

Cushman hesitated for a moment. "Everyone who made this voyage is very poor. The Leyden group who came over on the *Mayflower* brought their household goods, but these people own almost nothing."

The Governor stirred uneasily. "Surely they have pans and pots and weapons."

Cushman knew he had to be frank. "Most of them carry their worldly goods on their back."

Again Bradford looked out at the *Fortune*, a hard knot forming in the pit of his stomach. "I realize," he said carefully, "that a small ship of only fifty-five tons has too cramped a hold to carry most of the things we need. But every spade, every bucket, every keg of nails, and every saw will be useful."

"Pastor Robinson and I collected what few things we could," Cushman replied with a sigh. "They'll be brought ashore in the morning."

Bradford stared at him incredulously. "Surely our financial supporters have sent us tools and clothing and equipment!"

The glum Cushman shook his head.

Bradford made an effort to conquer his disappointment. "They're short-sighted fools." He forced himself to speak more cheerfully. "At least the food supplies will see us through the winter."

There was a long silence, then Cushman said, "They've sent no provisions, either."

The Governor's chair fell over backward with a crash as he jumped to his feet.

"I'm sorry, William. Pastor Robinson and I had no funds of our own to buy food for you," Cushman explained.

"Did you speak to the merchants?"

"Of course. I had several talks with Thomas Weston, who has taken charge as chairman. But he refused to spend another penny until the initial investment has been repaid."

"Weston isn't just a fool. He's mad." Bradford's temples pounded, and his throat felt dry and raw.

"How serious is the situation?"

It was impossible to explain to someone who had not lived through the terrible months of near-starvation. "We'll have to reduce the ration of meat and grain for everyone in order to feed thirty-five newcomers. This winter will be another nightmare." Bradford paused, then demanded, "Have you told me everything, or is there more?"

Cushman flushed. "I've saved the worst until last. The investors, Weston in particular, insist that they be repaid more quickly, and they want more furs and lumber."

"Are they mad?" Bradford demanded. "Have they no idea how difficult it is to keep body and soul together in the wilderness?"

"I'm afraid they don't know, William." Cushman tried in vain to placate his angry friend. "No one in all human history has ever lived as the people of this colony are living. How can the merchants visualize something beyond the scope of their imagination? I myself was stunned when I first landed."

"But you wouldn't be stupid enough to demand that we starve while putting money into your pocket!"

"Investors everywhere think of their own purses, nothing else," Cushman said. "And you know that Weston is greedier than most."

"If I had him here, I'd hang him!"

The gentle Cushman was stunned by his friend's violence.

"I've seen men and women die," Bradford told him in a harsh voice. "I've watched little children grow weaker, day by day, when there hasn't been enough to eat. Do you wonder that I have no patience with the Thomas Westons who think only of lining their own pockets?"

"Of course not." Cushman tried to speak diplomatically. "At the same time, I realize, as you do, that you depend on him and the other merchants for supplies. So you'll have to go along with them, at least to some extent."

"We'll do what we can," Bradford said curtly.

Cushman made a mistake. "And cut down on your own food production?"

"Impossible! New England is a land of plenty, and we've only begun to scratch the surface of her resources. But we can't earn a profit for others until we're able to keep body and soul together!"

He was so incensed that Cushman patted him on the shoulder in an attempt to calm him. "Do what you can, William. Or, if the burden is too great, you can always go back to Holland."

"Never!" Bradford didn't realize he was shouting. "We came to this new land because we wanted religious freedom. But that isn't enough. We aren't slaves, and we must support ourselves before we can repay our debt." Gradually he recovered from his outburst and, walking to a window that faced inland, stared out at the forest, the ever-present symbol of the wilderness. He — and every other settler — faced grim new challenges, but in one way or another they would be met. "Never fear, my friend. We're here to stay, and with God's help we'll survive. Freedom is indivisible. We won't be content until we're truly free — free of debt, hunger and fear."

The *Fortune* sailed off to England carrying a cargo of hardwood, sassafras bark for medicinal purposes and piles of beaver, otter and fox pelts. Fortunately for the peace of mind of the colonists, they did not learn for many months that French freebooters stopped the ship at sea and took the valuable merchandise.

Day-to-day existence at Plymouth was enough of a worry. The new arrivals soon discovered that the reality of New World living consisted of a constant struggle against the elements. Belts were tightened, and food supplies were eked out. The cold was ignored, and new houses were built. Each man was required to swear that he would uphold the Mayflower Compact, and all of the new arrivals were enlisted in the militia. With the coming of spring, hunting parties helped to ease the food shortage; but the lack of grain was critical, and the leaders of the colony were afraid that the months before the autumn harvest would be the worst they had ever known.

The settlers' problems were compounded late in May, 1622, when seven young Englishmen arrived in a longboat from a ship that was part of a fleet fishing off the coast about one hundred miles north. The news they brought was grave: they were the advance members of an expedition sent out by Thomas Weston to form a new colony in the area. Weston had written to the Pilgrims, and Governor Bradford was shocked to read that the financier had resigned from the group that was supporting Plymouth. If other members also withdrew, there would be no funds in the future for Plymouth's badly needed provisions, tools and equipment!

There was a near-riot when the settlers learned the news. "Throw Weston's spies out!" the hot-headed Stephen Hopkins demanded.

"Weston wants to starve us, so give his men no food or shelter!" Isaac Allerton shouted.

Elder Brewster disagreed. "These young strangers know nothing of the wilderness," he said. "If we turn them out, they'll be murdered by Indians or wander through the forest until they collapse. It isn't civilized to strike down the hands of those who raise their arms for help."

Governor Bradford ruled that Weston's men would be given a temporary haven.

The grateful young adventurers revealed that the captains of the fishing fleet were interested in the colony, and this information gave Edward Winslow an idea. He collected several bales of furs acquired in trades with the Indians, and the following day set out for the fishing fleet in the shallop, accompanied by eight men.

Two weeks later the party returned, and the shallop was riding so low in the water that two men bailed constantly. The whole colony gathered to watch and cheer as hogsheads of flour, barrels of pickled beef, mutton and pork, and sacks of dried beans and peas were carried ashore. The worst of the food shortage was over. There would be no feast, but Plymouth wouldn't starve.

That evening Winslow told the other leaders of the colony that the masters of the shipping vessels had refused to accept payment for the supplies. Each had generously contributed as much as he could spare, and although Winslow had insisted on giving them the furs in return, the pelts were worth only a fraction of what the food had cost.

Elder Brewster expressed the thoughts that were in the minds of everyone. "We made Weston's men welcome and have been feeding them, even though we've had nothing to spare. These gifts from the captains of the fishing fleet are the Lord's reward."

Even the nonchurch members could not deny that a miracle had taken place.

In August, 1622, two ships from England put into Plymouth harbor, bringing mail, no food — and sixty more of Thomas Weston's men. Weston himself wrote, insolently, that he was establishing his colony at the lower end of Massachusetts Bay, north of Plymouth. He had chosen the site, he said, because his followers would live near the Massachusetts Indians, who collected more beaver skins than any other tribe.

Weston's colonists were unruly brawlers who had been recruited from the slums of London. Many of the Pilgrims, afraid the newcomers would disturb the peace, wanted to send them on their way at once. But the leaders of Plymouth disagreed. "The Indians of New England," Governor Bradford said, "know these men are English, as we are. If they see brothers at odds, they'll make war against all of us."

The newcomers were allowed to remain until they could prepare for their journey to the land of the Massachusetts, and Plymouth's facilities were strained to the utmost. Householders who gave the young men shelter were dismayed when their guests kept the children awake half the night, gambling, roistering and cursing. The Londoners had enormous appetites, and as food was being rationed very strictly, they complained they were being deliberately starved.

They would do no work in return for the hospitality they were shown. They ignored requests to help build new houses, work in the fields or go out to sea with the fishermen. And they outraged the Separatists by playing cards and throwing dice on the Sabbath.

Their leader, Andrew Weston, the financier's younger brother, laughed contemptuously when Bradford asked him to keep his men under control. John Sanders, the second-in-command of the group, seemed to have a greater appreciation and understanding of the Pilgrims' position, but could do nothing to curb the excesses of the unruly mob.

Bradford called a meeting of the more responsible settlers at his house, but no one knew how to handle the problem. It was impossible, obviously, to place all the brawlers under arrest, for they actually outnumbered the adult male population of the colony. And an attempt to expel them by force would result in certain violence. No decision was reached, and it was agreed to meet again the following day.

John Alden and Edward Winslow left the Governor's house together. They walked toward the center of the town and, deeply engrossed in conversation, were startled when they looked up to find Andrew Weston and most of his men gathered in the Street.

The arrogant Weston blocked the path. "We want more food!" he shouted. "We know there are barrels of beef in your storehouse, and plenty of corn."

Winslow, always the diplomat, tried to make the Londoners see reason. "We give you no less and no more than we eat ourselves," he said. "If we empty the storehouse now, there will be nothing left before the harvest."

"You have a fishing boat," one of the newcomers called, "and you know how to find game in the forest. Give us the food in the storehouse!"

"We're hungry!" another added.

It was useless to tell these impetuous young men that everyone in Plymouth was hungry. Winslow and Alden exchanged uncertain glances as the crowd pushed forward, surrounding them.

"You're afraid of us," Andrew Weston said mockingly.

Winslow was tempted to draw his sword, but knew that a bloody riot would make matters worse. "I order you to disperse," he said, trying to speak calmly.

"We demand our rights!" Weston retorted.

Alden, a deceptively mild-mannered giant, entered the conversation for the first time. "What rights?" he asked pleasantly, hooking his thumbs in his belt.

The newcomers fell silent for a moment, then several became abusive.

"If you won't open the storehouse," Weston said viciously, "we'll break down the door and take what we want. You Separatists love to talk, but we want action."

Alden continued to smile. "It so happens that I'm not a member of the Separatist church, and I agree with you that this isn't a time for talk." He unbuckled his sword belt and handed the blade to Winslow. "Thank you, Edward. Be good enough to hold my coat, too."

Weston laughed a trifle nervously. "Just what do you think you're going to do?"

"I intend to remind you men that you're guests here and that you're expected to obey our laws."

Weston was amused, for everyone knew that fighting was strictly forbidden in the town. "Won't your Governor punish you if you fight with me?" he demanded mockingly.

"There will be no fight," Alden said quietly. "You see, it takes two to battle, and you won't touch me. I'm simply going to assert the authority of Plymouth in terms you'll understand." He lashed out sharply, and Weston staggered as the punch landed on his cheekbone.

Sanders caught his friend, and Weston, shaking his head to clear it, regained his balance. He leaped at his antagonist, swinging wildly and cursing. Alden ducked, planted a short, hard blow in the man's stomach with his left, and then silenced him with a smash that snapped his jaws shut.

Weaving groggily, Weston made another attempt to strike back, but missed. Alden landed two more jolting punches that rocked the man's head, first to the left, then the right, and suddenly the leader of the wild company slumped to the ground.

Alden, breathing easily, flexed his fingers, then nudged the body of the semi-conscious Weston with his toe. "Remove him!"

Two of the Londoners hastily obeyed.

"If anyone else wants to challenge the authority of Plymouth, I'm prepared to settle all differences of opinion here and now." Alden's gaze swept the crowd.

No one spoke or moved.

Alden took his coat and threw it over his shoulders. "I need ten men to chop trees." He jabbed his forefinger at those who stood nearest him. "You'll do."

"The rest of you," Winslow added, "will go out into the new field we're preparing. Stumps and rocks must be removed."

The Londoners fell in meekly behind the two Pilgrims, and neither Alden nor Winslow bothered to look back at them. The rebellion had been crushed.

10

A deceptive truce established a surface calm, and the newcomers from England were careful to obey Plymouth's laws and keep the peace. But on both sides resentment seethed beneath the surface. The colonists realized that the strangers would starve if turned loose in the forest; yet at the same time people resented giving them food. Everyone, women and children included, had less to eat because of the intruders' presence.

On the other hand, the young adventurers believed they had lost face in the showdown with John Alden, and several of the Londoners tried to goad Andrew Weston into striking back at the men who had made him look foolish. He needed no urging and, after learning the routines of daily living in the town, concocted a scheme designed to cause hard feelings between the Separatists and their powerful Indian neighbors, the Wampanoag.

It had become the custom of Hobomok, Sachem Massasoyt's ambassador, to spend a portion of each month at Plymouth and then return for a visit of a week to ten days with his own tribe. Weston learned of this arrangement and decided to put his plan into operation accordingly.

Hobomok ate dinner at the Governor's house with Bradford and Captain Standish on the evening prior to his departure on one of his regular journeys. During the hour or two that Standish's cottage was empty, Weston and one of his associates, a youth named Henry Johnson, searched it. They soon found where the Captain's heavy field armor, helmet and double-edged battle sword were stored.

Retiring at once to the quarters they themselves had been assigned, the pair waited until late in the night, when the whole town was sure to be asleep. Then they crept down the Street, past silent, thatch-roofed houses, and soon reached the Captain's house. Weston, displaying the stealthy skill of a professional burglar, silently entered the house while Johnson stood guard in the shadows outside. Standish was sleeping in the inner room, but the military equipment was stored in a leather chest at one side of the living quarters, opposite Hobomok's cot, and Weston went straight to it.

The lid creaked as he raised it. He paused, glanced at the *pinese* and smiled in grim satisfaction when he saw the Indian had not stirred. He took out the Captain's coat of chain mail, keeping it folded so the links would not rattle. Then he removed the breastplates and heavy helmet, took the sword from the box and carefully lowered the lid.

Laden with the stolen goods, he moved cautiously toward the door, hugging the equipment as he made his way slowly toward safety, one step at a time. A single glance over his shoulder reassured Weston that all was well. Hobomok was breathing evenly, deeply, and in a few more moments the task would be done. At dawn the Indian would leave for the town of the Wampanoag, and at some time during his absence Standish would discover that his property was missing. He would be sure to suspect the *pinese*, and recriminations would be exchanged. Feelings on both sides would harden, and before the incident ended, the haughty, self-righteous Separatists would be hauled down a peg or two.

Suddenly, just before Weston reached the door, Hobomok leaped from the cot, bounded across the room and tackled him.

The armor fell to the ground with a clatter. Weston groaned as the powerful Indian pinned him to the ground. And Johnson, hearing the commotion, realized that something had gone amiss and took refuge in flight.

"Captain, come," Hobomok called quietly, twisting Weston's arm behind his back.

Miles Standish entered in his nightshirt, blinking as he lighted a candle.

Weston immediately tried to bluster. "I caught this rascal trying to steal your sword and armor, Captain." It was difficult for him to speak with his arm held high behind him, and the words came out in a breathless rush.

Hobomok, who had gained enough mastery of English to understand what the Londoner had said, merely looked at him in scalding contempt.

There had been a time when Standish would have accepted the word of any civilized man in a dispute such as this, but he had learned to respect Hobomok, his friend. Red-faced, he glowered at the helpless man on the floor. "What were you doing here at this time of night, Master Weston, that enabled you to catch him?"

The glib Londoner was never at a loss for words. "I happened to see him examining your property earlier in the day, Captain. I was walking by the house at the time, and caught a glimpse of his face through the window. It occurred to me then that he intended to take the things off to this tribesmen friends in the wilderness. So I waited outside to catch him in the act. And I did."

Hobomok had too much dignity to reply to the charge.

Standish was silent for a moment. "Why didn't you come straight to me?"

The pain in Weston's shoulder and arm was excruciating, and he tried to wriggle free, but in vain. "He'd have denied it, and you wouldn't have believed me."

Standish made an attempt to curb his anger. "We'll have to take this whole matter to the Governor. Right now." He turned back toward the inner room to dress, calling over his shoulder, "Don't let him get away, Hobomok."

"Thief no escape," the *pinese* replied succinctly.

Less than thirty minutes later Governor Bradford had heard the story in his living room-office. His face expressionless, he said to the Londoner, "It would appear, Master Weston, that I must accept either your word or Hobomok's."

Weston's smile was coldly superior. "I dare say I can rely on you to dispense justice swiftly, Governor. My brother will be interested in the report I send him." He was indicating, in a none too subtle way, that Plymouth depended on the good will of the powerful Thomas Weston.

Bradford was not impressed. "Truth means far more to me than the opinions of your brother — or any other man. Hobomok?"

The *pinese* whipped a bone-handled knife from his loincloth and held the blade a fraction of an inch from Weston's throat.

The steel gleamed in the candlelight, and Weston shrank back on his stool. "He's going to kill me!"

"Maybe," Miles Standish agreed. "And I wouldn't blame him. You've made a serious charge against him, and it doesn't improve his disposition any to know that it's false."

"I suggest," Governor Bradford said calmly, "that you stop lying. As you can see, Hobomok's patience is limited."

Weston's bravado disappeared, and he stammered the plot he had concocted.

Bradford and Standish, exchanging occasional glances, were incredulous. "I wonder if you have any idea how seriously a dispute with the Wampanoag would jeopardize this colony."

Weston could not meet his gaze.

"Had your vicious scheme succeeded," Bradford continued in the same, even tone, "you'd have placed every member of this community in grave danger, including our women and children." He paused, then said sharply. "Tie him to the table, face down."

Weston struggled, but was no match for the sinewy Hobomok, aided by Captain Standish. They lashed him to a sturdy sawbuck table of pine, binding his ankles and wrists with leather thongs, which were fastened so securely that he could not move.

Bradford ripped away the Londoner's shirt and doublet, baring his back. "Hobomok," he directed, "bring me the whip that Massasoyt sent me as a gift. You'll find it in the bottom drawer of the chest in the next room."

Weston was terrified, but made a final attempt to put up a bold front. "You don't dare beat me," he shouted. "My brother will make you suffer if you touch me!"

"We are compassionate, and merciful," Bradford said, displaying no emotion. "Had you tried to embroil England in a war with one of her ancient enemies on the continent of Europe, King James would have ordered you hanged. I do not intend to hang you, but you must be taught not to deal lightly with human lives."

The *pinese* returned with the whip, an ugly instrument with a short handle attached to three broad thongs of rawhide. "Hobomok punish?" he asked eagerly.

"It seems to me it's his right," Standish said.

Bradford shook his head. All the natives of Cape Cod would lose respect for the people of Plymouth if a warrior were allowed to beat an Englishman. Even more important, a principle was at stake. "We're trying to establish a society in which justice is dispensed for its own sake. I can permit no displays of personal vengeance, even if they seem justified."

Hobomok was disappointed, but handed him the whip.

Bradford raised his arm, then brought the thongs down, hard, across Weston's bare back.

The Londoner screamed, shuddered and lay still.

The Governor struck him again, then raised the whip a third time. Had anyone told him, before he had left Holland, that he would be forced to perform such a distasteful duty, he would have deemed it impossible. But he had no choice, regardless of his personal sense of repugnance. Not only did Weston need to be taught a lesson he would remember, but his unruly associates had to be impressed, too, with the strict impartiality of Plymouth justice. The future of the colony made the punishment of a treacherous schemer an urgent necessity.

Shutting out the sound of Weston's sobs, Bradford dealt him nine strokes, then let his arm fall to his side. "Cut the prisoner loose," he said. "And send for Sam Fuller to put a poultice on his back."

Hobomok looked bewildered.

Bradford was too weary to explain that he felt no personal sense of satisfaction, that he had merely done his duty. It was difficult to prevent himself from becoming ill, but he had the consolation of knowing he had done what was right to protect the community he had been chosen to lead.

Weston's men were obedient but surly in the following weeks. Tensions remained high, and nobody was sorry when the interlopers went off to build a fort, at the southern end of Massachusetts Bay, on the site of an abandoned Indian village called Wessagusset. The citizens of Plymouth ruefully made an inventory of their shrunken food supplies, and their knowledge that the forthcoming harvest would be small added to their gloom.

The fear that the undisciplined rabble at Wessagusset would create troubles with the Indians haunted them even more than the realization that they would be forced to remain on short rations for many months. So Edward Winslow visited the sachems — or chiefs — of every tribe in the vicinity. He warned them that even though the men who were establishing their colony at Wessagusset were English, they were not the friends of the Plymouth settlers. He was greeted everywhere with skepticism, and in some places by open hostility. The natives could not believe that foreigners who had crossed the great sea from the same land were not related, and they were convinced that a trick of some sort would be played on them.

It seemed almost certain that there would be trouble, and Governor Bradford tried to brace for it. The palisades around Plymouth were strengthened, and as ammunition was short, men and women contributed lead buttons from their best clothes to make more bullets. A personal problem now occupied Bradford's thoughts, too: according to letters from England brought by the ships that had carried Weston's men to the New World, Alice Carpenter Southworth's husband had died in London. She, like Bradford, was now free to remarry.

He knew that he still cared for his childhood sweetheart, but was in a quandary. Life in Plymouth was harsh and demanding. Did he have the right to propose marriage to her, to ask her and her children to share privation and hunger? Bradford searched his soul, but could not find the answer.

Then pressing, immediate problems demanded his full attention. The harvest of 1622 was a dismal, frightening failure. There was too much rain, and only half of the corn crop matured. Peas and beans, barley and wheat rotted in the ground. Deer had moved to other grazing land, and only a few ducks and geese broke their annual flight south by pausing to rest on the ponds beyond the town's palisade. The Thanksgiving service was somber. Gloom turned to open despair when a heavily armed ship of two hundred tons, the *Discovery*, put into the harbor en route to England from Jamestown, Virginia. The vessel carried only enough food for her crew.

But a passenger, John Pory, former secretary of the Virginia Council, told the Pilgrims how Jamestown had solved a similar problem. The master of the *Discovery* carried large quantities of knives, mirrors, beads and other trinkets useful in trade with the Indians. He was willing to exchange these items for beaver, and the trinkets could then be used to barter with the Indians for provisions.

The people of Plymouth were asked to pay a high price in furs for the objects they wanted, but they proved that life in the New World had sharpened their wits. The captain of the *Discovery* needed planking, tar, water and medicinal herbs, and when the Pilgrims demanded an exorbitant fee from him, he promptly lowered the price of the trinkets. On that basis, a bargain was struck.

Bradford solved his personal dilemma and sent off a letter to Alice Southworth, asking her to marry him. Then, as soon as the *Discovery* sailed, he set out on an expedition to visit all of the Cape Cod tribes. Squanto and ten of the colonists, all heavily laden with trinkets, accompanied him.

Their fortune changed, and they met success everywhere. The natives sold them sacks of corn and beans, jerked venison and smoked fish in such large quantities that they had to employ native porters to carry the supplies to Plymouth. The Separatists in the group believed their prayers asking Divine intervention had been answered, and the whole party rejoiced.

Then, one morning, as the settlers were preparing to leave the village of the Monomoy, one of the most prosperous of the Cape tribes, Squanto suddenly became ill. He fell to the ground, moaning, and Sam Fuller discovered he had a raging fever. He was carried to one of the native huts that was hastily evacuated, and Fuller fed him a concoction of herbs from a wooden spoon.

The natives refused to approach the hut, where Bradford and Fuller were nursing the dangerously ill Squanto. Several of the other colonists came to them and said that, according to the local natives, he was suffering from the plague. No Indian ever recovered from the disease, they said, and anyone who remained near someone suffering from it would probably become infected, too.

Fuller and Bradford refused to abandon the Indian who had done so much to help Plymouth, however. Ignoring their own danger, they stayed close beside him for more than twenty-four hours. During that time he gradually grew weaker, and Bradford was unable to rouse him from a deep sleep. Fuller gave him a variety of medicines and herbs, but nothing helped. The other members of the party recklessly visited the hut during the long vigil, and even Stephen Hopkins, who was believed to be totally lacking in sentiment, had tears in his eyes.

At last Squanto stirred, and recognized Fuller, who was bending over him. "Where Governor?"

"Here." Bradford bent over the other side of the pallet.

133

The Indian looked up at him gravely but calmly. "Squanto die soon."

"No! We need you!" Bradford told him.

Squanto's lips curved vaguely in a fleeting smile, and he tried to shake his head, but lacked the strength. Then he closed his eyes and drifted off to sleep again.

A fire burning in a stone-lined pit in the center of the little hut threw off so much heat that the place was suffocating. But Bradford and Fuller shivered involuntarily. Without Squanto, Plymouth would stand completely alone.

Neither man was aware of the passage of time, and neither knew that several hours passed before Squanto opened his eyes again.

"Governor?" he whispered.

"I'm near you," Bradford said hoarsely.

"Pray for Squanto."

Bradford realized that the other settlers had crowded into the hut and were standing with lowered heads. "*I command thee this day to love the Lord thy God,*" he said, "*to walk in His ways, and to keep His commandments and His statutes and His judgments. And the Lord thy God shall bless thee in the land whither thou goest to possess it.*"

Stephen Hopkins, who had always scoffed at religion, said fervently, "Amen."

Squanto smiled, and his voice became stronger. "Now Squanto go to God of English in heaven," he said, and fell back onto his pallet.

His breathing became so faint that none of the men in the hut knew the precise moment when he died.

A grave was dug for him, and his body, wrapped in a blanket, was lowered gently into it.

The Separatists did not believe in religious ceremonies to commemorate death, but the settlers could not leave Squanto without paying him a final gesture of respect. Their reserves of gunpowder were scanty, but they unhesitatingly loaded their muskets, then stood in military formation on both sides of the grave. Bradford raised his sword above his head, and when he brought it down, the point touched the head of the grave. There was an instant's silence, then the roar of gunfire echoed through the still forest.

The members of the expedition wept openly as they left the village of the Monomoy. Many had died since the *Mayflower* had arrived in the New World, but none had contributed more to the welfare of Plymouth than Squanto.

Fuller, the last to depart, turned for a moment, then plodded after his companions. Now, more than ever before, the men of Plymouth had to rely solely on themselves in a menacing, alien world.

11

Plymouth's old foe, the weather, became her worst enemy again in December, 1622. Frigid winds roared in from the north, snowstorms from the west blanketed the little settlement, and Atlantic gales buffeted her. But her people had developed a resilience that enabled them to survive. Adversity had tempered the men and women who had been so helpless when they had first come ashore from the *Mayflower* twenty-five months earlier. Even the fainthearted had learned to laugh at hunger and danger, and no one ever mentioned the thought of returning to England or Holland. The blessings of freedom were more valuable than wealth.

No one wasted energy or time. Firewood was cut on high ground that would be used for the coming spring planting, making it unnecessary to fell those trees later. Food acquired by the expedition trading with the Indians of Cape Cod was distributed as it arrived, and each family was made responsible for its own. Whenever the weather permitted, everyone worked outdoors. The men continued their never-ending task of building new houses, and even on the coldest days the fishermen went out to sea.

The New World had changed a group of undistinguished farmers and artisans, shy housewives and ordinary youngsters into pioneers capable of overcoming any obstacle. The odds against success remained high, but the settlers unanimously believed they were in New England to stay. They had learned to work together, helping one another. Knowing they could rely on no outside assistance, they stood united, ready for any new emergency.

They did not have long to wait. Early in January, 1623, an Indian arrived from Wessagusset with a letter written by John Sanders. The colony on Massachusetts Bay, Sanders said, was starving, and the men were victims of a deliberate conspiracy against them. Neither the powerful Massachusetts nor any other neighboring tribe would sell them corn at any price. So they had boarded up all the entrances to their tiny community except one, and were preparing for war.

Sanders declared he had already warned the Indians that if they refused to trade with him, he would take the food he needed by force. He assumed, he said recklessly, that Plymouth would join with him in his campaign. Oddly, he made no mention of Andrew Weston, who was supposedly in command of the settlement.

The alarmed leaders of Plymouth gathered at Governor Bradford's little three-room house, and the Massachusetts warrior who had brought the letter was called in. The brave admitted that Sanders had paid him to act as a messenger, but said he came only to warn Plymouth. "Hear now the words of Wituwamat, sachem of the Massachusetts," he intoned solemnly. "If the strangers who live now in the huts at Wessagusset make war against the Massachusetts with their thundersticks, all foreigners in this land will die."

Plymouth's worst expectations had been realized. Thanks to Weston's men, the Pilgrim colony was in danger of being attacked by a tribe strong enough to send hundreds of warriors into battle. If that should happen, the Cape tribes would be eager to share in the loot, and would join the other savages.

Edward Winslow wrote Sanders a letter worded in the strongest terms. "We altogether dislike your intention," he said bluntly. "You can expect no help from us in this rash venture or any other foolish scheme. You must know by now that you cannot *force* the Indians to trade with you. We gave them blankets and knives and mirrors in return for food. Why can't you do the same? We know you have such supplies. Use them, and above all, use your heads — or you will surely lose your lives."

Bradford, whose patience with Weston's band was exhausted, added a final paragraph to the letter. "When we have been in danger of starvation," he said, "we have lived for weeks at a time on groundnuts, clams, mussels and other foods near at hand. Rather than bring about your certain ruin by waging an unjust war, scour the beaches and forests for edibles. Remember there are only a few of you, while the Indians are as numerous as the trees of the wilderness. Be sensible!"

The Massachusetts warrior was given a hot meal, gifts for his sachem and a blanket for himself. After he had gone, the leaders of Plymouth relaxed, telling each other that Weston's followers would, in all probability, calm down and behave sensibly. But Captain Standish did not share their optimism.

"I don't trust that rabble at Wessagusset," he said, "any more than I trust the savages."

There was no reply to the Pilgrims' letter, and tension eased, but a new cause for alarm arose less than two weeks later. Hobomok, who was spending the winter with his own people, arrived unexpectedly at Plymouth with word that Massasoyt was dying and wanted to say farewell to his English friends before he joined his ancestors.

Governor Bradford and his friends realized that the peace with Plymouth imposed by the strong chief of the Wampanoag on the lesser tribes of Cape Cod would collapse if Massasoyt died. Then these nations would be tempted to join forces with the wrathful Massachusetts and make a determined effort to destroy both Plymouth and Wessagusset. The Pilgrims' future looked bleak.

Edward Winslow and Sam Fuller volunteered to make a journey to the main town of the Wampanoag, where they would try to save Massasoyt's life. Standish pointed out that, if they failed, they might be murdered by the enraged warriors of the tribe. But they believed it was necessary to take the risk, and virtually the whole colony saw them off.

They found Massasoyt suffering from a fever similar to that which had killed Squanto. But Fuller believed he had learned something about the disease now.

"Wrap him in blankets," he said, Winslow translating for him into the language of the Wampanoag. "Make him warm in the heaviest, thickest blankets that the people of Plymouth gave to you as gifts."

The members of the chief's family obeyed, and Fuller went to work, mixing a concoction of powders and herbs that he carried with him in a kit that had become his most precious possession. Some of the drugs had come with him from Hollands, roots had been laboriously gathered from the forests of the New World, and a few of his dried leaves and berries were used by the Indians themselves.

He shook small amounts of the contents of several vials into a tiny bowl of hardwood and, with several Wampanoag nobles watching him curiously, ground the herbs and roots into a fine powder. These he poured into a gourd, adding boiling water, and walked to the bough bed of the patient.

"Tell him to drink, Edward," Fuller said.

Winslow looked dubious.

"Hurry. The longer we wait, the more bitter the brew will become."

Winslow translated the order to Massasoyt. One of the Sachem's squaws raised the patient's head, and he drained the contents of the gourd, choking and making a wry face.

"I hope you realize," Winslow said, "that our lives won't be worth a ha'penny if he dies. The whole tribe will believe we've poisoned him."

Fuller reacted with the calm of a man who had done his duty and had a clear conscience. "That," he said, "is a risk we must run."

Massasoyt drifted off into a deep sleep. Winslow went hunting, at Fuller's suggestion, and shot a large, plump duck. He made a strong broth; Massasoyt drank quantities of the hot soup every few hours through the rest of the day and night. Shortly before dawn his fever broke, but Fuller insisted that he swallow several more doses of the medicine.

Within twenty-four hours the Sachem seemed completely recovered. "Massasoyt, the great eagle of the Wampanoag, will always be the friend of his brothers in Plymouth," he assured Winslow.

The two settlers remained in the town of the Wampanoag for two more days, and only when it seemed unlikely that Massasoyt would suffer a relapse did they agree that the time had come for them to leave. They paid a farewell call on the chief, and found him sitting on a chair that vaguely resembled a throne, with a crude representation of an eagle cut into its high back above the Sachem's head. Massasoyt was still weak after his illness, but he had dressed for the occasion in his best fringed shirt and wore a headdress made of freshly dyed, multi-colored feathers.

Winslow and Fuller approached the chair and, careful to observe Indian custom, raised their right hands, palms held outward, in formal greeting.

Massasoyt's eyes were sharp and alert, but he glanced at his guests just once in what appeared to be acute embarrassment. Then, saying nothing, he stared out into space over their shoulders. His nobles and the other braves who stood behind him were silent, too, and appeared thoroughly ill at ease.

Winslow realized something was amiss, but his manner was smooth. "The men of Plymouth will rejoice," he said, "when they hear that Massasoyt, son of the eagle and grandson of the moon, is restored to good health."

The silence in the lodge was strained, heavy.

"What's wrong, Edward?" Fuller murmured.

Winslow shrugged, then glanced questioningly at Hobomok, who stood on his chief's left. The *pinese*'s expression was stiff, his eyes guarded.

"Massasoyt thanks the men of Plymouth for their help," he said in his native tongue, then added quickly in English. "Go now. Hobomok follow."

Fuller and Winslow were bewildered, but had learned they could trust Hobomok. They raised their hands again in formal gestures of farewell, and were not reassured when Massasoyt, even more obviously embarrassed than he had been a few moments earlier, inclined his head a fraction of an inch but continued to avoid their gaze.

The two settlers left at once, pausing briefly at the hut in which they had slept to collect their muskets and other belongings. Shouldering their packs, they went out into the forest, where they walked more slowly down the trail that would take them back to Plymouth.

A dark figure glided out from behind a tree a few yards ahead of them. Winslow raised his musket, but let it fall again when he recognized Hobomok.

The *pinese* looked around anxiously to make certain he was alone with the settlers, then said in a low voice, "Massasoyt sad. Want to be brothers with English. Know English save his life. But not betray other tribes."

Winslow felt a chill moving up his spine. "What's happened?" he demanded.

"When Massasoyt sick," Hobomok replied somberly, "chiefs of Massachusetts decide to make war on Plymouth."

The gentle Fuller whistled softly under his breath. "Can't he persuade them to change their plans?"

"Too late," Hobomok replied grimly. "Other tribes of Cape agree to help in war. Before Massasoyt better, chiefs of other tribes give word to Massachusetts. If no keep word now, no join ancestors when die."

The situation was even worse than either of the Englishmen had feared, and they looked at each other bleakly. "Can you tell us anything about their plans?" Winslow asked.

Hobomok hesitated, wrestling with his conscience.

"You are our brother for all time," Winslow said firmly.

The *pinese* drew in a deep breath, then exhaled slowly. "In half-moon," he declared, "many warriors attack Wessagusset. Burn, scalp, take slaves and prizes."

That meant, the colonists realized, that the war would begin in just two weeks.

"When Wessagusset gone, all tribes fight Plymouth." Hobomok raised his hand in farewell and disappeared into the forest.

The crisis was urgent. "What can we do?" Fuller wondered.

"By ourselves, nothing. We'll have to take immediate action of some sort, but the decision is up to the Governor and Captain Standish. All I know," Winslow continued, setting a rapid pace on the trail, "is that we have no time to lose!"

The pair hurried home with the alarming news, and the men of the colony held an emergency meeting at the Fort. Captain Standish wanted to take the initiative and strike first, but Governor Bradford was more conservative, hoping a way could be found to preserve peace. The settlers argued both sides of the case, then the Governor cut short the debate.

"As the elected head of this colony," he said, "I must assume ultimate responsibility." His voice became crisp. "Captain Standish!"

"Sir?" Miles Standish stood at attention.

"I want you to sail to Wessagusset immediately."

A slow, thin-lipped smile spread across the Captain's wind-burned face.

"The Indians are like children," said Bradford. "When a small boy misbehaves, he's spanked to teach him the error of his ways. The savages need to be taught a lesson, too, and you'll be their instructor. Do whatever you find necessary to end this threat to our security."

The men sat forward on the hard benches, listening anxiously.

"I don't believe I can take enough men with me in the shallop to conquer the whole Massachusetts tribe," Standish said, frowning.

"We aren't strong enough to launch a full-scale attack under any circumstances," Bradford replied. "If you find the Massachusetts have attacked Wessagusset before you get there, send word to me and I'll dispatch all the reinforcements we can spare."

Standish nodded, then was silent for a moment, pondering. "Suppose the Massachusetts are still biding their time, and haven't yet attacked."

"In that case," Bradford declared, "try to persuade their sachem, Wituwamat, to behave reasonably."

"You ask too much, sir."

"Perhaps I do." The Governor's voice became harsh, strained. "When we've hunted for wild game in the marshes, we've watched whole flocks take fright and fly off after we've killed only a few birds." He gazed intently at the Captain.

Standish nodded. "You may rely on me to do my duty," he replied, saluting.

The meeting was adjourned, and every settler in Plymouth knew that, one way or another, there would be bloodshed.

The beach at Wessagusset was deserted, and no guards were stationed on the colony's pinnace, which rode listlessly at anchor. The wintry silence of the wilderness enveloped the harbor.

Miles Standish, standing in the prow of Plymouth's shallop as it sailed slowly toward the shore, glanced around at the nine settlers who had accompanied him. "It may be that we're too late," he said softly.

The men all started talking at once, conjecturing about their chances and the possibility of ambush.

"Quiet!" Standish said sharply. He had selected the roughest men in Plymouth for the nasty task ahead, and they were less well-disciplined than more considerate men. "I'll give the orders and you'll obey them." He measured a charge of gunpowder into the pan of his musket, and fired the weapon into the air.

There was a tense wait, and finally three figures emerged from the forest. Gaunt and dressed in rags, they made their way slowly and painfully down to the water's edge.

"They're Englishmen!" one of the settlers in the shallop announced triumphantly.

"We'll go ashore at once," Standish said.

When the boat moved closer to the beach, four men jumped into the icy water and pushed it up onto the sand. Standish, his armor clanking as he climbed out of the shallop, looked in astonishment at the pathetic Londoners who had been so insolent and aggressive when they had first arrived at Plymouth from England.

The Captain wasted no time on unnecessary greetings. "Why aren't sentries posted on your pinnace?"

"We're the sentries," one of the men replied. "We were in the woods, looking for groundnuts." He shivered, then added bleakly, "There's nothing in the woods except snow."

Any member of the Plymouth militia who abandoned his post would be punished, but Standish had not come to Wessagusset to teach Thomas Weston's hirelings military fundamentals. "Have the Massachusetts attacked your town?"

"Not yet," the man replied with a listless shrug, "but we expect them to come any day."

"If we're lucky, maybe we'll escape in the pinnace," one of his companions added. "Or maybe it will be better if the savages kill us. Being scalped is better than starving to death." He looked at Standish, and a faint gleam appeared in his eyes. "Are you bringing us food?"

The Captain found it hard to curb his temper. "We have only enough for our own needs," he replied curdy. "But we've brought you something better than food."

The trio lost all interest in the newcomers.

"Where is your town?" Standish demanded impatiently.

"See them elms back of the evergreens?" One of the Londoners pointed with a thin, grimy hand. "It's there."

The Captain left two men to guard the shallop, instructing them to fire a warning shot at the first sign of danger. Then, accompanied by the rest of his squad, he made his way up the beach and through a small patch of woods to a clearing. Thomas Weston's followers had tried to copy the fortifications they had seen at Plymouth, but lack of intelligent planning, combined with sloppy execution, had produced negligible results.

The palisade was, at best, a flimsy fence. Not only were there several gaps in it, but the men who had built it had chopped down absurdly small trees in order to make their own work less arduous. As a result, anyone could climb over the stakes with ease. The creaking, poorly constructed gate was open and unguarded, and the compound inside consisted of two ramshackle wooden buildings and a number of native huts made of clay.

John Sanders came to the entrance of the larger house, and the Plymouth settlers, remembering him as a large, sinewy man, were shocked. His cheeks were sunken, his skin sallow and wrinkled, and there were dark smudges under his eyes. His stained, torn clothes hung loosely on his body, and he straightened himself with an effort as he recognized the new arrivals.

"Welcome to Wessagusset," he said sardonically. "Have you brought us corn?"

Standish was surprised to discover he felt sorry for the wretches. By sharing the rations he and his party carried, they could give the ravenous Londoners one or two meals. "We have a little." It was painful to see the slow smile appear on Sanders' cracked lips. "Where is Andrew Weston?"

146

"He died last month." Sanders raised a hand limply, then let it fall to his side again. "Maybe it was two months ago. I can't remember. And I don't care."

"Then you're Governor? I want to confer with you."

"I'm honored. Come in and let me show you the Governor's mansion."

The Captain left his squad in the compound and followed Sanders into the house. Never had he seen a dwelling so miserably furnished or in such a state of disrepair. In spite of the cold there was no fire burning in the crude hearth, which was piled high with ashes. Two tables had been made of rough planks, and empty barrels served as stools. Several mounds of soggy reeds and evergreen boughs appeared to be pallets, and Standish shuddered.

He concentrated on the business at hand. "We've learned that the Massachusetts are going to attack you, and we've come to punish their leaders before they can strike."

A beaten man, Sanders put his hands over his face for a moment. "You can't stop them. There are as many natives in these parts as there are flies in summer."

His bleak despair revolted Standish. "How many members of your colony are still alive?"

"There were thirty-four who answered roll call this morning. But I don't know how many will disappear today or how many will vanish tonight."

The Captain was aghast. "Do you know what has happened to the men who haven't come back?"

Sanders spread his hands in a helpless gesture, then dropped them wearily.

"The savages have killed all of them?"

"No, we've found the bodies of a few who have died in the forest, but we've been too weak to bury them."

"When I've finished my work here," Standish said, speaking gruffly to hide his sympathy, "I'll take you and your band to Plymouth. It's plain you can't stay here. Our people will make you welcome if you'll accept the terms of our Compact and obey our laws."

Sanders rubbed a hand across his bony face. "We've had enough of the New World. I want to go home, and so do the others."

The Captain gestured impatiently. "Only expert seamen could sail your pinnace across the Atlantic."

"We know our limitations. But we think that with luck we can reach the fishing fleet off the Maine coast. We don't expect charity from the ships' masters. We're willing to work for our passage."

"Why haven't you sailed before now?"

"We've been afraid the Massachusetts would launch their attack if they saw us making preparations to escape." There were tears in Sanders' eyes, and he brushed them away with the back of his hand. "We've been trapped here by the savages. They've been playing a game with us, you see. They have scouts watching us day and night."

"Are there Massachusetts scouts out there in the forest right now?" Standish asked.

"Of course."

"That makes my task easier." The Captain went to the door and called to one of his men, Thomas Rogers, the youngest member of the group, who was familiar with the native languages. "Rogers, go out yonder and shout to the Massachusetts in their own tongue. Tell them I demand to see Wituwamat at once."

Sanders looked at Standish incredulously. "You've really come to save us," he said incredulously. "You're leading an advance party."

"No, there are ten of us who make up the entire expedition."

"How can a small patrol make war against a whole tribe?"

Standish knew it would be a mistake to reveal his specific plan of action to someone as unreliable as Sanders. So he changed the subject abruptly. "Tell your men we'll feed them now," he said, and walked out of the foul-smelling cabin into the open, where he inhaled the crisp, clean air.

He took as much food from his company as each of the squad could spare. The news that there were corn and jerked venison to eat spread quickly, and Sanders' men came out of their huts, their eyes enormous as they watched. Soon others appeared from the dark forest, and by the time the Captain began to distribute the supplies, he found he had twenty-six mouths to feed. Every scrap disappeared, and he had to revise his earlier estimate. There would not be enough left to give the men of Wessagusset anything more.

One of the band, his mouth stuffed with corn, suddenly jumped to his feet in alarm and pointed toward the forest. Rogers and a tall, husky warrior in a fur cape were walking toward the palisade, and he hurried to the broken gate to meet them. The brave refused to enter the compound, and several of the Plymouth settlers reached for their blunderbusses.

But Standish stopped them. "Put away your firearms," he said softly. "We don't want to frighten him."

Rogers announced that the warrior was a *pinese* of the Massachusetts named Peksuot.

"Why has Wituwamat refused to obey my command?" the Captain asked imperiously, deliberately speaking in English, although he now understood the native dialects. It might be advantageous, he thought, to pretend he didn't know the native language.

Rogers dutifully translated; then the *pinese* replied in a haughty tone. "The sachem of the Massachusetts obeys only the god of thunder who is his father."

"My business," the Captain declared, "is with Wituwamat."

There was avarice in Peksuot's voice as he said, "The little *pinese* of the English wants to buy skins of beaver? Let him know this. The Massachusetts will not trade skins for knives and beads. They will take only fire-sticks."

Standish pretended to shrug helplessly, and knew from the Indian's reaction that he had won the upper hand. "I will deal only with Wituwamat," he repeated stubbornly. Then, as a seeming afterthought, he added, "I suppose he's afraid to meet me here."

The warrior was stung. "Wituwamat will come," he said, and raced off into the forest.

The Wessagusset men crowded around the Captain, asking questions simultaneously, but he refused to answer them. "Sanders," he said, "I'm borrowing your house. Follow my orders, all of you, and with luck you'll sail before sundown tonight to join the English fishing fleet." He paused, waiting for the last murmurs to die away. "Go to your huts and stay there until I give you permission to come out again. That's all I want you to do. Go now."

The Londoners were confused. But, too weary to argue, they found it easier to obey.

Standish examined the outside of the house, and was satisfied when he saw that the two windows, which were covered with oiled paper, were so small that even an agile, slender youth could not climb through them. The building had only one room and a single entrance, so his confidence increased as he turned to his squad.

"I selected you for this mission," he said, "because none of you will shrink from the unpleasant work that must be done if Plymouth is to survive." He glanced at the men, and saw that Thomas Rogers looked uneasy. Two of the burly settlers, John Crackston and Moses Fletcher, were relaxed and smiling, however. "Rogers, join the sentinels at the boat." It would be wrong to let anyone who might hesitate remain in the house.

Rogers seemed relieved as he hurried off to the beach.

"Wituwamat," Standish told the others, "will probably bring a large number of warriors with him. That means we'll have to entice him into the house. If any braves come in with him, we must treat them as we deal with him."

Crackston, a heavy-set stonemason, laughed savagely. "I'll take care of Wituwamat, Captain. I promise you I'll put my first shot through his head."

"No!" Standish declared. "We can't use firearms or the Massachusetts will tear down the walls of this flimsy place."

Moses Fletcher, who had been a blacksmith in London, pulled off his stocking cap and scratched his head. "We can't use our muskets and pistols?" He sounded shocked.

"Only as a last resort," Standish replied firmly. "All of you carry knives, and all of you have two hands."

Crackston smiled grimly as he looked down at his thick, strong fingers and calloused palms.

"You've volunteered for the most important task," the Captain told him, "and you shall have it. But remember, if the sachem escapes, we can expect terrible reprisals."

"He won't," Crackston said grimly.

"I'll help him," Fletcher added. "I give you my oath, Wituwamat and his ancestors will be reunited before nightfall."

Standish turned to the others. "You'll act as reserves," he said, "and serve where needed. All of you have been London street brawlers in your time, so help where you can."

Blunderbusses were loaded and hidden under pallets, and pistols were concealed behind barrels. The Captain unbuckled his sword belt, then shoved the blade under a pile of reeds. At last everything was in readiness, and the squad went out into the open again. The men stood in tense silence, waiting, occasionally stamping their feet on the frozen ground.

Time dragged, but at last they saw a large party of Indians emerge cautiously from the forest.

"There must be twenty-five or thirty of them," Fletcher muttered.

Standish stared at a thick-chested warrior with a scar on the right side of his face that caused his mouth to droop in a permanent sneer. He had met the arrogant Wituwamat on several trading expeditions, and saw that the sachem recognized him, too.

The Indians halted at the rickety gate, and the Captain beckoned imperiously. The warriors halted, however, and several of them spoke earnestly to their chief, obviously trying to persuade him not to enter the compound.

Standish deliberately laughed loudly, contemptuously. Wituwamat responded to the challenge. Followed by four of his warriors, he walked slowly toward the house — and the ambush that had been prepared for him.

12

The beaver cape thrown over Wituwamat's shoulders swayed slightly as the sachem of the Massachusetts walked toward the house. Directly behind him came Peksuot and two mature, powerful braves, all carrying bone-handled knives in their belts. Bringing up the rear was a younger warrior, a man in his early twenties, also armed with a knife. The other members of the Indian party waited at the flimsy gate.

There was unconcealed hatred in Wituwamat's eyes as he drew closer, but he raised his arm in a formal greeting. "The sachem of the Massachusetts, the son of the thunder," he intoned, "wishes to know why the men-from-across-the-sea have invaded his land."

Standish raised his own hand, returning the greeting, and said, "Wessagusset is a town of the English. It is not a part of the land of the Massachusetts."

Not realizing that the Captain understood him, Wituwamat turned to Peksuot, and speaking in the dialect of the Monomoy, said softly, "Before another night comes, there will be only scalps and ashes at Wessagusset."

The knowledge that the Indians intended to kill and burn hardened Standish's resolve. "It is too cold to talk in the open," he said, rubbing his hands together. "I invite the sachem of the Massachusetts into the house."

Wituwamat and Peksuot made no attempt to hide their disdain for the seeming weakness of the foreigner. But they followed him into the building, as did the other three braves. The Plymouth settlers were ranged around the room, and all were poised. In this moment of crisis, no one lost his head. Standish stationed himself just inside the door.

"The Massachusetts want fire-sticks," the sachem declared in an arrogant, brittle voice. "They will not trade beaver for cooking pots that squaws use."

"What will the Massachusetts do," Standish demanded, his tone rasping, "if the English refuse to trade fire-sticks for beaver skins?"

"The Massachusetts will take the fire-sticks, and send the men-from-across-the-sea to join their ancestors. There they will need no beaver." Wituwamat glared first at the Captain, then at the other colonists.

The open threat was sufficient cause to begin the fight. "Now!" Standish shouted in English, slamming the door and bolting it quickly.

The next half-hour was a bloody one as Indians and whites engaged in hand-to-hand combat. The sachem and three of his warriors were killed; the youngest of the braves managed to break free and dashed out into the compound. In full view of the waiting party, Standish took careful aim with his knife, then hurled it at the fleeing brave. The blade buried itself in the Indian's back, and he pitched forward and lay still.

The warriors retaliated with a shower of spears and arrows, and now the colonists fired. The roar of the muskets echoed through the forest. Frightened by the noise and the smoke that hurled out of the blunderbusses, the Indians panicked, then ran. The brief battle was over.

Standish called to Sanders, and the men of Wessagusset came out of their huts. "Take the bodies of the Indians we've killed," the Captain directed, "and pile them outside your stockade."

When they were finished, Standish called them together again. "If I were you," he said, "I'd scalp them. And if the

Massachusetts send any braves back here to take away the casualties, catch the rogues and hang them."

Sanders gasped.

"In war," the Captain told him, "the object is to inflict as much damage on the enemy as you can while suffering as little as possible yourself. The Massachusetts wanted violence, and we've given them a strong dose. When a savage goes into battle, the only language he understands is force."

Sanders muttered that he and the rest of his band would leave on their pinnace as soon as they could collect their belongings.

"As you will," Standish replied. He refrained from adding that New England would be a better place without Thomas Weston's followers.

Several of Weston's men tried to thank Standish, but he cut them short. He led his own squad down to the beach, and did not speak again until the shallop had pushed off and her sail was filling. Then he glanced back in the direction of Wessagusset and sighed. "We'll have no more trouble with the Massachusetts or their friends, I'm sure," he said. "This has been a nasty day's work, but Plymouth is safe."

William Bradford sat quietly behind his desk, listening to Standish's account of what had happened at Wessagusset. The Governor was pale, but managed to exert great willpower in order to compose himself.

The Captain completed his recital and leaned back in his chair. "We've put such terror into the barbarians that not one tribe will dare to attack us now. Mark my words, we're going to have an era of real peace."

"Real peace." Bradford's voice was heavy as he repeated the words.

Standish was puzzled.

"I can't help but think of the Lord's commandment, *'Thou shalt not kill.'*"

The Captain smiled grimly. "You know the Bible better than I do. But there's a line in it somewhere to the effect that those who live by the sword will perish by the sword. The Indians started something, and we finished it."

The Governor could not disagree. "Oh, I know, Miles. It was either kill or be killed. I feel ashamed; yet at the same time I realized we had no choice. I can only hope now that the other tribes won't seek revenge and that the Massachusetts won't seek reprisals. The next few days will tell the tale."

Forty-eight hours after Standish and his squad returned to Plymouth, a large party of Massachusetts warriors appeared at the gates of the town. They had brought their squaws with them to prove they did not intend to wage war. Bradford received them at the Fort and accepted their promise to live for all time as friends of Plymouth.

As a final gesture the Indians offered the settlers five bales of prime beaver as a gift, but Bradford refused to accept the pelts. "We want to trade with you fairly," he said. "But we can't take bribes. Wituwamat was killed because he wanted to murder us. But we bear no grudge against your nation. Our good will can't be bought, but we give it to you freely."

Even though the supplies of food in the storehouse were still limited, the Massachusetts were given a meal before they left. They were thoughtful and silent as they departed, and Edward Winslow declared that the savages had learned a new concept of justice.

News of the incident at Wessagusset spread rapidly through the wilderness. The Cape tribes wasted no time, and they, too, sent delegates to Plymouth to renew their pledges of peace.

For the present, at least, the danger to the colony had been reduced.

The rest of the winter passed slowly, and spring came late to Cape Cod in April, 1623. Bradford was elected for a third one-year term as governor, and surprised the men by insisting that everyone accompany him to the storehouse. He unlocked the door, then pointed to the bags of corn, beans and peas inside.

"There," he said simply, "you see our future. I intend to use all of the grain and vegetables as seed."

The settlers stared at one another in astonishment, and Stephen Hopkins was the first to find his voice. "What will we eat between now and the autumn harvest?"

"We must redouble our efforts to live off the land," Bradford replied. "Everyone who can be spared will go hunting and fishing. We'll close the school so the children can gather shellfish and berries and groundnuts."

"I suppose," Hopkins retorted, "that you want us to eat the herring we catch in Town Brook, too."

"Certainly not," the Governor replied severely. "Every last herring we catch will be needed for fertilizer."

Several of the men began to grumble.

Bradford raised his hand for silence. "We've jumped from one crisis to another ever since we came to the New World," he said. "We need stability — and a permanent, steady food supply. Now, while there's nothing to fear from the Indians, we have our chance. Only once, for a single season, have we had enough to eat. If we miss this opportunity, we may not gain another."

A number of the settlers stared at him in surly silence.

"If you prefer to live from one week to the next, sometimes from one day to the next, that's your privilege. In that case, however, you'll have to get someone else to lead you. Now that you know what's in my mind, I'm willing to resign. But if I remain as governor, I must look beyond the present and do what I think best for our permanent welfare. I leave the decision to you."

There was a strained silence; then Stephen Hopkins, who had been the first to rebel, stepped forward. "I was wrong," he said. "We've learned how to tighten our belts, and we can do it again. I suggest that we show our confidence in Governor Bradford — and in ourselves."

The vote was unanimous, and Bradford remained as governor.

More than ever before, the citizens of Plymouth dedicated themselves to the hard task that awaited them. From the beginning of their venture they had submerged their personalities, their individual desires for the common good. They obeyed their leaders — the Governor, the Captain and the Elder — because they knew that only through an application of the strictest self-discipline could the colony survive.

It had not been easy for the men and women who had come ashore from the *Mayflower* to put aside all thoughts of personal happiness. Men had postponed the building of the large, comfortable homes they and their families wanted, and instead had hunted, fished and farmed for all, surrendering everything they had caught and grown so that all would be able to share the meager provisions.

Now, in the time of supreme crisis, the discipline that Plymouth had known from the outset began to bear fruit. The experiment, in which everyone gave all of his time and all of his effort to the community and its needs, succeeded beyond the hopes of the men who were directing the efforts.

Bradford and the other farmers had planted more than two hundred acres, using every kernel of grain and every vegetable seed. On the day the herring began to run, even the hunters stayed at home. The fish were scooped up in buckets, kettles and other containers; then the herring were buried in circles around the plants, as Squanto had prescribed.

Guards were posted to prevent wolves from prowling through the fields at night, and the community was so free of fear that the boys began to take a share of sentinel duty. Gentle, steady rains fell at least two days each week and encouraged even the most fearful. The diet of fish and meat, relieved occasionally by a few berries and nuts, was monotonous, of course. People missed cornbread and the favorite dish of the youngsters, a bean and pea pudding flavored with chunks of venison. But no one complained.

"We have every reason to hope that our gamble will succeed," Bradford declared one day late in May. "If it does, Plymouth will become self-sufficient at last. Beginning at harvest time this autumn, we and our children, and their children after them, will never need food from England again."

The settlers were tired every night, but they had cause to feel satisfied with their efforts. Gradually it dawned on them that they were no longer fighting the wilderness. They had learned the ways of the New World. They understood the forest and the sea. The wind held no terror for them, and they were afraid neither of the rain nor of the lightning overhead when a storm raged. They had come to terms with the frontier and rightly regarded it as their home.

Animal skins were cured, and householders spent their free evenings making moccasins for their families. Needles were scarce, so they borrowed a custom of the Wampanoag and used porcupine quills instead. Women sat beside their hearths

159

after dark, plaiting reeds with such dexterity that they made shirts for their sons and dresses for their daughters out of the strong grasses that grew beside ponds. Fish oil was refined and reduced for use in lamps, and one of the girls discovered that a soft, sandy clay found on the shores of a little inland lake made an excellent soap.

Ears were beginning to appear on the tall cornstalks, bean and squash vines were sturdy, and the grapes and berries were becoming plump. Cranberries filled the marshes and, for the first time, the wheat was flourishing. Even the children, who were tending the leeks and watercress, were raising an unusually large crop.

"There is every hope," the Governor said in an announcement, "that we will become self-supporting by autumn."

The rains had stopped in mid-June, and the sun burned in a cloudless blue sky. No one was concerned, however, and the men believed that rain would come again in good time. Then a few ears of corn began to ripen prematurely, vines started to wither and berry bushes became brittle. Suddenly a sense of deepening crisis pervaded the settlement.

Some of the younger men tried to water their fields by carrying buckets from Town Brook. But the earth was so parched that water vanished immediately beneath the surface, and the crust became hard and cracked again. The experiment in irrigation was a total failure.

By late July the situation had become so serious that Governor Bradford called an emergency meeting of all citizens. "With good fortune and hard labor," he told the men, "our hunters and fishermen can keep us alive until harvest time. But if there is no harvest, we can't survive another winter."

"You're a farmer," Isaac Allerton said. "What can we do to save our crops?"

"Nothing," the Governor replied bleakly.

The men followed Governor Bradford now on his daily inspections, and each morning they asked fearfully, "Have the plants died?"

"No," he said. "Not yet. There's still hope."

But that hope dwindled rapidly. The dry spell continued, and at the beginning of August there was still no rain. The sacrifices of two and one-half years had been made in vain, the settlers said gloomily. Even the more courageous were ready to give up. At almost any hour of the day, someone could be seen listlessly gazing out to sea, hoping a ship would appear to take everyone back to England and Holland.

Some of the bravest lost their courage. Others tried to keep their own spirits and those of their neighbors high, but they were fighting a losing battle. Many who were not members of the Separatist church now came to Sabbath services at the Fort and joined wholeheartedly in the prayers offered by Elder Brewster. Others merely said, "It's no use. We're doomed."

The children, so long accustomed to grinding hardship, lost hope, too. "What do we say to our little ones," mothers asked the Governor, "when they tell us they're hungry?"

He shrugged, unable to offer counsel in this hour of peril. "Feed them until the food supplies are exhausted," he replied.

But there were some who did not waver. Each evening, an hour or two after sundown, Susanna Winslow could be heard singing her children to sleep. Her voice, sweet and clear, rose softly on the hot summer nights, and those who heard her held out at least a shred of hope that the famine would be averted.

Miles Standish took refuge in rough humor. "I sent off a letter to Barbara in England," he said to Isaac Allerton one day. "I actually asked her to come over and marry me. Now I think I'd do better if I joined her there — but I don't think I have the strength to swim quite that far."

Stephen Hopkins tried to joke, too. "I've eaten nothing but fish for so long," he said, "that when I go out to sea in the shallop, cod and halibut leap out of the water to greet me as their brother. What's more, I think they're right. I believe I'm actually beginning to grow scales."

But one man could not force himself to jest.

Governor Bradford felt impotent, helpless. Unable to sleep, he spent most of his nights pacing restlessly on the beach. He became gaunt with deep creases beneath his eyes. Unlike some of his friends, he could not resign himself to the seemingly inevitable catastrophe. Occasionally Edward Winslow and Miles Standish tried to comfort him, but he was inconsolable.

"Plymouth must not die," he said fiercely. "If we fail, where can men go if they want to worship in their own way? If we perish, religious freedom will expire with us. That cannot be. It must not be."

But the weather remained dry. No rain clouds appeared at any time. The stars shone brightly every night, and when dawn came, the sun rose again, red and glowing. By the end of the first week in August, Bradford knew that if the drought was not broken in the next day or two, it would be too late. The precious corn and wheat, the nourishing beans and squash would crumble into dust. And in a few months the settlers would starve.

One evening, unable to eat the lobster and mussels that young Thomas Cushman had boiled, the Governor walked stiff-legged to the rocks overlooking the beach. He had sought refuge and solace there after Dorothy had died, after the raid on the Massachusetts and during many of the colony's other crises. Although he didn't know precisely why he always came to the same place, he felt instinctively that this spot was his true home. From the crest of the largest rock, he could look out across the harbor. Turning, he could see the town and beyond it the wilderness. This was the Plymouth he loved.

Now, in desperation, he realized that all men were feeble, impotent creatures. Only Divine Providence was powerful, he thought, and recalled one of his favorite Psalms. He stood, bowed his head and spoke aloud, softly but distinctly.

"I will lift up mine eyes unto the hills, from whence cometh my help.

"My help cometh from the Lord, which made heaven and earth."

He straightened, breathed deeply and, climbing down from the rocks, made his way back toward the town. In spite of his exhaustion there was a spring in his step as he walked quickly up the Street. He halted at Elder Brewster's house, unmindful of the late hour, and pounded at the door.

After a short wait the old man appeared, tugging at the tie of a faded dressing gown. "What's wrong, William?" he asked in alarm.

"A great many things have been wrong for far too long a time," Bradford replied.

The Elder lit an oil lamp and led his guest into the small living room of the cramped house. He stared at his protege, saw his flushed face and bright eyes, and wondered if he were ill.

"I scarcely know where to begin." The Governor was too excited to take the chair his host offered him, and paced up and down the room. "For weeks the solution of our problem has been right there, waiting for us to see it. But we've been too blind."

Brewster nodded, but said nothing.

"We've watched life draining out of our plants and vines, and we convinced ourselves there was nothing we could do to save them. In our wretched stupidity, we neglected to turn to the one source of all good."

A faint smile appeared on Brewster's weathered face.

Bradford looked at him sharply. "You've known it all along. Why have you kept silent?"

"I'm not an ordained clergyman, but there's one thing I know." Brewster sat forward in his chair, his hands clasped over a knee. "People can be exposed to truth, but until they recognize it for themselves, they can't be forced to see that it exists. I've given hints, strong hints, in my sermons. But no one has taken them."

"Would you have allowed us to starve?" the Governor demanded.

The old man inclined his head. "I would have had no choice. If a man loses his soul, what can he gain?" Suddenly he smiled and, rising to his feet, extended his hand.

Bradford looked at him in awe. The Elder would have been willing to see his wife and sons die, to lose his own life, for the sake of principle. Knowing it would have availed Plymouth nothing for him to impose the solution, he had waited patiently for someone to understand what needed to be done.

"My instinct tells me," Bradford said, "that everyone must take part."

"I believe you're right," the Elder replied. "There must be no exceptions. We will succeed only if all our people speak with one voice."

Bradford hurried off to his own house. He went to his desk, wrote a few sentences on a sheet of parchment and, after sanding the wet ink, called to the lad who lived with him.

"I've written a proclamation, Thomas," he said. "I want you to take it to every house. Read it aloud at each, so no one will fail to know what I've said. I have decreed that tomorrow will be a special holy day.

"Our people will gather outside the Common House at sunrise and will march together to the Fort. All of us, men and women and children, members of the Separatist church and non-members, will pray together for Divine help. No one will work, and anyone who fails to attend will be banished from Plymouth for all time."

The boy, wide awake now, snatched the parchment and ran off down the Street.

Soon lamps were burning in many of the houses as families discussed the Governor's dramatic act. Several of the men who were not Separatist gathered at the Common House, where they held a brief meeting. Bradford, a few doors away, could hear the sound of loud voices, and smiled.

He was not surprised, a short time later, when Stephen Hopkins knocked at his door. "Come in, Stephen," he said. "I've been expecting you."

Hopkins stalked angrily into the room. "William, I want to protest. I have no faith in the powers of prayer, nor do some of the others."

"I understand." The Governor remained calm.

"You have no right to command us to take part in your ceremony. It's one thing to order members of the church to attend, but—"

"I know what you're going to say, Stephen," Bradford interrupted. "I'm violating the terms of the Compact. Affairs of church and state are not being kept separate."

"Exactly!" Hopkins clenched his fists and rocked back and forth on the soles of his worn boots.

"I admit the charge," Bradford said. "But this is a time of unprecedented peril, and I must follow the dictates of my own conscience. I believe we'll be helped only if every one of us prays with all his heart and soul, might and main. If you call me unfair, I plead guilty. If you call me a dictator, I concede that you're right." He stood, his expression solemn, and faced his angry visitor. "This is the most important hour in all our lives. Never have we known one like it, never will we experience another."

Hopkins remained unconvinced. "I still refuse to take part," he said flatly.

The Governor accepted his challenge. "Very well. I'll excuse you, Stephen, on one condition."

Hopkins' eyes narrowed.

"Suggest an alternative. Tell me something else we can do, and I'll follow your advice."

"You know that's impossible, William! If I were capable of creating rain, I'd have done it long ago. I can't work miracles!"

"No, but God can," Bradford replied gently. "I'll see you tomorrow morning, Stephen, at the services."

13

Drums rolled as the first streaks of dawn appeared in the sky, and people hurried from their homes, dressed in their best Sabbath clothes. No one spoke. Even the youngest children sensed the solemnity of the occasion and silently clung to their mothers' hands. After a short wait, Bradford appeared with Standish and Brewster. The drums sounded a slow, rhythmic beat, and the citizens of Plymouth followed their civil, military and religious leaders to the Fort.

Bradford opened the service by explaining its purpose. "I have no way of knowing whether our prayers will be effective," he said. "But I beg you to give yourselves without reservation to the task before us." For an instant his gaze met that of Stephen Hopkins, sitting in the front row. "In this terrible time of need, we know we are lacking in wisdom and strength. Let us throw ourselves humbly before the altar of the Lord and ask Him to show us His mercy."

Elder Brewster moved to the pulpit, and Bradford quietly took a seat on a bench in the second row. Brewster delivered a sermon that lasted the better part of the morning, then asked for a volunteer to lead the congregation in prayer. A dozen men jumped to their feet, and the Elder called each to the pulpit in turn.

The services did not end until sundown, when the exhausted settlers returned to their homes. They had touched no food or liquid all day, and at the Elder's request would not break their fast until morning. Sam Fuller had suggested that girls and boys under ten years of age be allowed to eat, but Brewster had refused. Everyone, regardless of age, was required to demonstrate a willingness to humble himself. Strangely, none of the children whined or cried. They seemed to understand the spirit of the occasion better than their parents realized.

Most people retired early, but Governor Bradford went to the rocks, intending to remain there all night. He had barely settled himself when he heard someone climbing up to the top of the boulder, and saw Stephen Hopkins in the bright moonlight.

Surprisingly, Hopkins was neither brazen nor belligerent. "May I join you, William?"

"Of course." They sat in silence for a time.

"I never knew there were so many stars," Hopkins said gloomily. "The sky is filled with them."

The reflection of the moon on the sea hurt Bradford's eyes, and he covered his face with his hands.

"If we're lucky," Hopkins said after another silence, "perhaps a ship will pick us up."

"I suppose." Bradford felt completely drained.

"My wife and daughter were asking my plans just before I came down to the beach. It's strange," Hopkins mused, "but I've made none."

"Neither have I. The prospect of becoming a clothmaker in Holland again has no appeal to me." Bradford spoke softly, but his voice echoed hollowly across the empty beach.

Hopkins suddenly lost the last of his bravado. "I — I have no desire to go back to England. My son has no future there. Neither do I."

The Governor looked at him. "What will you do, Stephen — assuming, of course, that a ship comes for us?"

"I want to stay here." Hopkins pounded the rock with his fist, then crumpled and began to weep.

Bradford caught his arm and, unable to speak, pointed at the sky. Two small clouds, the first anyone had seen in many weeks, had appeared overhead.

Hopkins raised a trembling hand to his mouth, and his eyes widened as another cloud materialized, then still another.

The two men watched in growing wonder as dark masses blew in on a gentle breeze from the sea. A long time passed, and around midnight the stars and moon completely disappeared. A rumble of thunder sounded in the distance, and Bradford was unable to swallow.

They stood, looking at one another uncertainly. The thunder grew louder, then a flash of lightning streaked through the sky. Hopkins gasped and hid his face for an instant in his patched sleeve.

A few raindrops spattered the rocks. Then the heavens opened, and a steady rain began to fall.

The two men continued to stand on the rocks. Their clothes became drenched, but neither of them knew or cared. Bradford's humility was so overwhelming that he could feel no joy, no sense of triumph.

"My family and I," Hopkins said at last, "will join the church tomorrow. I have, with my own eyes, witnessed a miracle."

The rain fell every night for ten nights, and every day the sun appeared. The parched earth soaked up the moisture, and gradually the plants came to life again. The corn revived quickly, and stalks of wheat stood erect once more. The vines of beans and squash became strong, and the many vegetables turned green. On the eleventh day, after the rains stopped, Bradford made a careful inspection of the fields, and that evening announced that more than ninety-five per cent of the season's crop had been saved.

The miracle was demonstrated in other ways, too. Never had there been so many fish in the sea, and the men landed huge cod and tuna. John Alden put the carpenters and coopers to work making new barrels, and all of the remaining supplies of vinegar were used to preserve the enormous catches. Several of the children stumbled onto a treasure of birds' eggs, and the colonists enjoyed the first omelets they had tasted in years. Then, almost anticlimactically, Isaac Allerton succeeded in domesticating several young wild *turkies* the boys had captured. Within a year, he said, every household would have its own fowl in backyard pens.

People still hungered for many things, of course. The diet remained monotonous and would not be relieved until the harvest. Many longed for beef and white bread, and the younger children looked blank when their parents told them that someday they would drink milk. Clothes would not last through another winter, and there was a shortage of thread.

Then the Governor revealed the secret that he and Allerton had kept: gunpowder and bullets would be exhausted in the early autumn. But no one was worried now, and Captain Standish placed no restrictions on the powder and ammunition the hunters carried into the forest.

"A way will be found," the settlers told each other, serenely confident. "For the moment we lack many things, but we'll soon have them."

The Fort was crowded on the last Sabbath in August, and virtually all of the colonists who had not been members of the church now joined. Stephen Hopkins expressed their sentiments when he rose from his seat in the congregation and said, "We know, as do few on this earth, that the Lord is generous and good. We will remember all our days that He has blessed us."

The excitement subsided gradually, and by the last Friday in August everyone had returned to normal work schedules. Then, literally out of the blue, the *Anne* and the *Little James* sailed into Plymouth harbor, bringing relatives and friends — and a greater store of provisions and supplies, cloth and hardware and gunpowder than anyone had dared to want.

No one would every forget the exciting morning of the ships' arrival. When the *Anne* was first sighted on the horizon, the sentries were afraid she might be a French man-of-war. As the men gathered in the Fort, others thought she might be a pirate vessel. Fears increased when the smaller *Little James* was sighted, too.

"It isn't possible," the colonists told each other breathlessly, "that two merchant ships could be coming here together. We're going to be attacked! This means war!"

Governor Bradford alternated between hope and a firm resolve to repel invaders. Captain Standish, responding to the emergency with the calm of a professional military man, prepared for the worst. Members of the militia were mustered, women and children were ordered to the Fort for their own protection, and the gates of the palisade were closed and barred.

The huge cannon that overlooked the harbor was loaded, and everyone waited tensely. Only Elder Brewster was serene. As he said later, he found it impossible to believe that Plymouth could have survived the cruel drought only to be destroyed by alien invaders.

Suddenly the red, white and blue flag of England rose slowly, majestically to the *Anne*'s topgallants. For a hushed instant the news was too good to be true. Then, all at once, people began to laugh, cry and shout. Children threw off all restraints and, almost for the first time since they had come to the New

World, could be children again. Men forgot their dignity as they raced down the rocks to the beach, the women close behind them.

Newcomers stood on the decks of the two ships, waving energetically as the ungainly wooden craft sailed into Plymouth harbor. Then, as the passengers came ashore, there was bedlam. Husbands who had been separated from their families for years wept unashamedly as they greeted their wives and children. Youngsters from Holland and England, grown almost beyond recognition, hugged their parents. Sisters and brothers and cousins exchanged almost inarticulate cries of joy as they were reunited. Miles Standish cast aside all dignity as he enveloped his future bride, Barbara, in a bear hug.

Governor Bradford was so frantically busy that he had no chance to visit his childhood sweetheart, Alice Carpenter Southworth, until evening. She was staying at the house of her sister and brother-in-law, Priscilla and William Wright, who had come to Plymouth on the *Fortune*. Another sister, Juliana Carpenter Morton, and her husband, George, a leader of the Separatist community in Leyden, had also been aboard the *Anne* and were staying with the Wrights, too, so the house was crowded.

It was impossible for Bradford and Alice to exchange any private words there, so he offered to show her the sights of the town, and they wandered together into the Street. There was bedlam everywhere. Householders had taken in relatives, friends and strangers. Mattresses had been placed in the Fort for the single men who had come to the settlement on the *Anne* and *Little James*. A work crew laboring under John Alden's direction was building an addition to the Common House, several temporary storage sheds had already been erected, and a frantic Isaac Allerton was supervising the loading of stores and other cargo. Stephen Hopkins was measuring the ground behind the Common House, where several large, permanent storage buildings would soon rise, and needed the Governor's advice.

Allerton rushed up to Bradford. "William," he said, "I can't draw up revised work schedules by tomorrow. We'll have to wait at least a day or two before we assign tasks to the new men."

The Governor disagreed. "That would be a waste of talents. I feel particularly encouraged because there are several carpenters and stonemasons among the immigrants. We need them at once, obviously."

Allerton stared at him hopelessly. "But I can't make work schedules when I expect to be spending the night checking off items of merchandise as they come ashore."

Bradford glanced apologetically at Alice. "I'll do the schedules myself, Isaac."

They were interrupted by a group of the newcomers, who approached them hesitantly. "Governor," one asked, "when may we make our applications for land?"

"I'll have to study the needs of each family," Bradford replied, "and then I'll assign lots for houses and farmland beyond the palisades. Of course," he added as an afterthought, "we'll have to clear several hundred acres of forest before the new agricultural land can be used."

"Is it true, Governor," another wanted to know, "that all of us will be enrolled in the militia?"

"We'll call a meeting sometime tomorrow and explain the requirements of citizenship," the harassed Bradford said.

Alice stood beside him, waiting patiently, a steady smile on her face.

Two or three men clamored simultaneously. "Governor, is it true, sir, that everyone must join the Separatist church?"

"Certainly not!" Bradford said emphatically. "Men are free to worship as they please. However, as this settlement was founded by Separatists, we are allowing no church here other than our own — for the present. You're welcome to attend our services whenever you wish, but no one will force you to come to them. And if you disagree with our theology, you may worship in your own home."

"Governor, the Mayflower Compact—"

"I shall read it to all of you tomorrow," Bradford replied in a weary tone, "and you'll be obliged to accept it if you want to stay here. It grants citizenship to those who are willing to abide by our laws and who will accept the principle that church and state are — and must remain — separate."

"I have two children, Governor," one man said. "One is a boy of eleven, the other a girl of nine. When will my wife be allowed to enroll them in your school?"

Bradford removed his hat and ran his fingers through his hair, a gesture that reminded Alice of a habit formed in his youth. She smiled, recalling that it was a sure sign he felt crowded.

"We provide free education for all children here," he said, "but we're going to need additional volunteer teachers to take care of the enlarged classes." Grasping Alice by the elbow before others could question him, he started off again down the Street.

"I don't envy you your responsibilities," she murmured.

"I accept them willingly, but I can't do everything at once!" He paused before a door. "Would you like to inspect my house? There isn't much to see, but at least we'll have a few minutes to ourselves."

She nodded. "I'd like it very much, but I feel guilty when so many people need you."

"They'll come after me again soon enough," he declared, opening the door.

Alice walked slowly from room to room and tried to hide her dismay. Never had she seen a place so bleak, so barren. There were no rugs on the floors, not even braided rushes. Priscilla had made curtains for her windows out of scraps of material, but the windows of the Governor's house were bare and ugly. Not one ornament decorated the walls, and it was evident that every item of worn furniture was intended for hard use. This was obviously the home of a bachelor, a place totally lacking in softening touches.

William, she thought, had changed, too. His face was lean, his muscles rippled beneath his shirt, and his eyes, his very bearing, reflected the confidence of a man accustomed to giving commands — and being obeyed. The eager, idealistic boy she had known in Yorkshire was gone, and in his place stood a man who was a stranger to her. The thought frightened her.

Bradford was studying her, too. Alice was even lovelier than he had remembered, and the maturity he saw in her face gave her a new and wonderful dignity. Yet there were invisible barriers that separated them and made him feel ill at ease. Her marriage to Edward Southworth and the tragedy of Dorothy's death were complications far more subtle than he had imagined when he had written to her.

"Why have you come here?" he asked abruptly.

Alice returned his gaze steadily. "Because I want to find myself. I'm anxious to learn all there is to know about Plymouth. I want to find out everything I can about life here. I — well, I've lived for a long time in London, and I'm not certain, within myself, that I could be happy so far from the only kind of civilization I've ever known."

"That's wise," he heard himself say.

"For your sake — and mine — and the sake of our children, I don't want to make any mistake." Alice hesitated for an instant, then plunged on. "It's plain that you're going to be very busy in the next few weeks. The new people need you as much as those who came before us. So, while you devote your time and energies to them, I'll have an opportunity to get my bearings."

Bradford reluctantly agreed. "I suppose you're right," he said, and even though he wanted the question of their future settled, he knew that patience would be their best protection.

The first days of September were chaotic, but Governor Bradford and his lieutenants, working night and day, soon established order. The most immediate task was the building of houses for the newcomers, but the problem was handled so deftly that the immigrants were incapable of imagining how much the original settlers had suffered. John Alden took charge of the project, of course, and used the services of every man who had worked as a carpenter or stonemason. There was no shortage of manpower now, and others went to work in the forest, cutting down trees, then shaping them into planks.

The Common House was enlarged, and as its cellar was too small to accommodate the supplies of ammunition and gunpowder, a new munitions depot was raised. It was the first structure in Plymouth to be made exclusively of stone. Two new storehouses had to be erected, too, and the perishable supplies were not brought ashore until safe storage space was available to house them.

The settlers realized that their debt to their financial supporters had multiplied, so everyone worked harder to reduce it. Timbers of prime wood were cut and loaded in the hold of the *Anne*. Fur-trading missions visited the Wampanoag, the lesser tribes of Cape Code and the Massachusetts. They were able to offer the Indians such valuable items as axes with metal heads now, and came home with huge piles of beaver, otter and fox. They brought bales of deerskins, too, which the women cured.

There was no longer any doubt that the colony would be able to pay off its debts. Bradford and Allerton believed that the last of them would be discharged within two to three years. Then Plymouth would no longer be forced to depend on outside help, and the settlers would be in a position to buy what they needed with their own money.

Some of the veterans believed that the *Little James* was the most precious of all the new assets that had been acquired. Hopkins and his shallop crewmates went out to sea for a day in the pinnace, and returned in triumph. Their catch was four times larger than any they had ever brought in, and everyone knew that in the future there would always be more than enough fish to eat. A ship capable of crossing the Atlantic under her own sail certainly could be used to explore up and down the coastline. And plans were already in the making for Winslow and Standish to make a visit, in the spring, to a Dutch colony off to the south called New Amsterdam, which was located at the mouth of a river discovered by an explorer named Henry Hudson.

The women were grateful for an oddly shaped contraption in the cargo, a spinning wheel. Alden used it as a model and, in his spare time, began to fashion others like it. Housewives could look forward with confidence to the day, in the immediate future, when they could make their own linen cloth out of wild flax. Then, when sheep were imported, they would not be forced to rely on the Old World for wool.

The men who had been joined by their wives and children were supremely happy, and the newcomers were initiated into the mysteries of the forest and the sea. Everyone in the colony attended the wedding of Miles Standish. And people agreed that, after his lonely years as a widower, he deserved a bride as lovely and charming as his Barbara.

One man had no opportunity to rejoice, however. Governor Bradford, driving himself unmercifully, worked from dawn until the small hours of the next morning. Nothing was done without his consent, and people came to him in a never-ending stream for advice and help. He literally had no time to himself.

He was so busy he failed to realize how quickly the weeks were passing. Captain Peirce announced, late in October, that he intended to sail for England in ten days. Bradford was stunned when Priscilla Alden came to him and told him, in confidence, that Alice Carpenter Southworth was thinking of returning to London. Then, at last, the Governor knew he had reached a turning point in his own life.

Alice Southworth stood in the entrance of the house, the home of the relatives with whom she was staying, and her smile was steady. "Good morning, William," she said.

Bradford bowed a trifle awkwardly. "Will you come for a walk with me?"

"Of course." She went into the house, got her cloak and joined him in the brisk autumn sunshine.

Bradford led her down the Street toward the beach. "You must be very angry with me, and I can't blame you," he said abruptly. "I've neglected you shamefully."

"You've had your duty to perform," she replied calmly. "I've wondered how you stand the strain. I've never known anyone to work so hard. Everyone says that if it weren't for you, Plymouth would have floundered long ago."

"People exaggerate." He flushed, then waved aside two of the newcomers, whose expressions indicated they wanted advice of some sort. "There are a half-dozen others waiting at my house. I'm afraid this is one day they'll have to wait."

They did not speak again until they reached the rocks, where he helped her onto the heavy boulder. Bradford spread his short cape for Alice, and for a few moments they watched several of the immigrants who had been given the task of searching the beach for shellfish. "This is my favorite spot, and I wanted to share it with you," he said, then turned to her suddenly. "Is it true you're planning to go back to England on the *Anne*?"

"I've considered the possibility," Alice replied carefully, "but I've made no definite decision."

"By now," he said, "your mind should be made up. You should know whether you think you could be happy in the New World."

Her expression did not change. "I've reached a decision."

He was frightened by the realization that she was thinking of returning to England. But life at Plymouth had taught him to fight for what he wanted and believed right, to ignore odds and overcome obstacles. "Will you marry me?" he demanded fiercely.

"Yes, William. Of course," she said gently.

Bradford was bewildered. "Then why were you thinking of sailing?"

"You hadn't proposed to me — in person, that is. I know you've been dreadfully overworked, but I thought it just barely possible that you might have changed your mind since I asked you for time to think."

He stared at her, then grinned, and suddenly his face looked young and fresh.

Alice smiled, and a moment later both of them were laughing joyously.

The Governor of Plymouth took a single step forward and embraced her in full view of anyone who happened to be glancing in their direction. Neither cared, for their kiss was a promise of the good, rich life that awaited them. Bradford could feel Alice trembling, and was himself deeply shaken.

The long, hard years were at an end. Never again would he know loneliness, the empty sensation of a man who worked so hard for the happiness of others while finding none in his own life. They would bring her sons and his to Plymouth, and in time would have children of their own, too.

The seeds of freedom that the Pilgrims had planted had taken root, and future generations would reap the benefits of the sacrifices made by the early settlers. Life would not be easy in the centuries that stretched ahead, of course. Bradford had learned, as those who were to come after him would learn, that freedom was a precious plant requiring constant attention. It had to be nourished and protected, guarded at all time if men were to reap its fruits.

The coming of the *Anne* and the *Little James* marked a milestone in the development of Plymouth and of all the New World, for from that time forward the colony at Cape Cod was secure. Ships came and the rich produce of America was sent in an ever-increasing stream to England and Europe. The newcomers learned, as had the original settlers, to live in peace and friendship with the Indians.

Plymouth was not destined to become a great city, a major political or industrial center. It was the original New England colony, the first settlement, but it was much more. The Pilgrims' separation of church and state became a fundamental American tenet, respected by all faiths. Their concept of citizenship grew into the universal suffrage that is a cornerstone of American democracy. Their dedication to religious tolerance remains a sacred heritage. Their idea of universal military conscription was later adopted by a great nation in times of national danger. And their system of free public schooling became the birthright of every American child.

The codes and principles of a little band of realistic idealists who built a crude village on the edge of a wilderness left indelible marks on the land that was to develop into the United States of America.

BIBLIOGRAPHY

Bradford, William (with Winslow, Edward). *A Relation, or Journall, of the Beginnings and Proceedings of the English Plantation settled at Plimouth in New England*, by "G. Mourt," London, 1622-23.

———. *Of Plimouth Plantation*, London, 1664; complete edition published in Boston, 1856.

———. *William Bradford his Booke*, 1652. Manuscript in library of Massachusetts Historical Society.

New England's First Fruits, 1643. Author unknown; believed to have been written, at least in part, by Edward Winslow.

Arber, Edward. *The Story of the Pilgrim Fathers*, Boston, 1897.

Goodwin, John A. *The Pilgrim Republic*, Boston, 1888.

Hutchinson, Thomas. *History of the Province of Massachusetts Bay*, Vol. 1, London, 1765.

Plymouth Colony Records, Vol. 1 and 2, Boston, 1861.

Plymouth Town Records, Plymouth, 1889.

Thacher, James. *History of the Town of Plymouth*, Boston, 1832.

Willison, George F. *Saints and Strangers*, New York, 1945.

Winsor, Justin. *Narrative and Critical History of America*, Vol. 3, Boston, 1889.

A NOTE TO THE READER

If you have enjoyed the novel enough to leave a review on **Amazon** and **Goodreads**, then we would be truly grateful.

The Estate of Noel B. Gerson

Sapere Books is an exciting new publisher of brilliant fiction and popular history.

To find out more about our latest releases and our monthly bargain books visit our website: **saperebooks.com**